LOVE IN THE GOLDEN SUN

It's 1877 in outback New South Wales — bushranger country. After the new school teacher, feisty Grace Stevens, has her stagecoach robbed by enigmatic bushranger Major Midnight, she's determined to unmask him. Grace is torn between her attraction to Midnight and repulsion at what he does. However, the Major may not be all he seems. The two of them must learn to trust one another before romance can blossom, while solving a conspiracy that threatens the future of Australia ...

ALAN C. WILLIAMS

◆

LOVE IN THE GOLDEN SUN

Complete and Unabridged

LINFORD
Leicester

First published in Great Britain in 2021

First Linford Edition
published 2022

A catalogue record for this book is available
from the British Library.

ISBN 978–1–4448–4939–4

1

It was going to be one of the most mem-
orable days of my life. I would record it
in all of its bone-jarring, dust envelop-
ing detail when I wrote my memoirs this
evening.

*On September the eight in the year of
Our Lord, one thousand eight hundred and
seventy-seven, I travelled on the road to my
new home in Jerilderie.*

I needed to recall every facet of this
journey. There were four of us seated on
the least comfortable of benches in this,
supposedly Mr Cobb and Co's latest and
finest coach. It would be a seven-hour
journey from Narrandera to Jerilderie,
seven hours of torture on a track that
jarred every bone in my body. It was
evident that our driver was intent on
steering our coach over every rock and
rut upon this cow track that some come-
dian had chosen to call a road.

Another bump sent me crashing into

1

Mr Arthur O'Shane. Once again, I apologised though it was not my fault. In furious exasperation, I half stood to lean from the window.

'Oi you, driver — you missed that boulder! Better luck next time!' The driver must have heard me over the rumbling of the wheels and galloping horse hooves as he turned, gave me a toothless smile and nodded.

My fellow passengers stared as I resumed my place. 'What?' I asked, angrily.

Mrs Drummond, supposedly a veteran of this journey through the outback, tisked and muttered about unbecoming behaviour for a young lady.

'Mrs Drummond. I am on my way to Jerilderie to help educate the children there. If I were a lady, I would not have chosen to leave the civilisation of Sydney Town for a posting in the Outback. No other teacher has agreed to go to the ends of the earth. So there.'

The Reverend Peabody gave me a smile and a polite clap. Like me, it was

2

his first journey to the back of beyond. His reasons for doing this were different from mine. His was to do the Lord's work in 'taming the savage heathens' of Jerilderie as well as providing succour to those of the flock who'd had no preacher for this past month. The previous churchman was sorely wounded and had passed a week later without waking up. Mrs Drummond had mentioned that it might have been the work of a bushranger in those parts, Mad Charlie Michaels.

'It does appear that our driver is intent on breaking the speed record for this journey, Miss Stevens,' The Reverend observed. We were travelling much faster than ten miles an hour. I tightened my bonnet, concerned it might blow off through the open window.

'It's because of the money we're carrying, I expect. I heard the driver talking to his shotgun at the last change of horses. This is sadly like the wild west of those states in the Americas. The thought of a great deal of cash brings out the worst in men.' Mr O'Shane had spoken little thus far on our journey.

It was apparent that the bank at Jerilderie required funds and the stagecoach was the most sensible way of getting it there. There was no reason to believe security was so lax that any bushranger would be aware of this special shipment. Nonetheless, the driver was taking precautions.

I peeked out of the windows on both sides. It was approaching noon, a pleasant enough spring day. There was little apart from the pale green leaves on gum trees dotted amid the wheat-coloured grass. The land was flat to the point of monotony, nothing changing as the stagecoach thundered along. Sheep munched away, oblivious to us, yet the occasional kangaroo appeared, bounding along in an imaginary race with our transport. Eventually, it became tired of the game and left us to gallop on.

Not for the first time I wondered what had possessed me to travel to this isolated township miles from anywhere. My father was in Sydney, my mother long deceased. I had no one to keep me there in our state's capital, no betrothed. Why then travel to a town barely twenty years old and more than four hundred miles from my former home? The answer was simply my spirit of adventure, unusual in a woman and even more so when I, Grace Mary Stevens, was scarcely nineteen years of age. It was a thrill to be doing the same as those pioneering explorers of New South Wales and the other states of our vast continent, names like Ludwig Leichhardt, Burke and Wills. They were European pioneers who'd crossed the Great Dividing Range west of Sydney and opened up this vast continent to others, the searchers for a new way of life.

Of course, the aboriginal peoples had been here long before. From my meagre research on the area, there was a group who called themselves the Wiradjuri who occupied much of southern New South Wales west of the Great Dividing Range. I'd never met an aboriginal . . . at least thus far.

Mr O'Shane produced a flask from the inside of his coat jacket. He unscrewed the top, rubbed it on his less than clean sleeve then offered it around. No one accepted his offer.

'What none of you? Best whisky, it is. Put hairs on yer chest . . . oh, not you, Miss Stevens.'

Mrs Drummond folded her arms in disgust and stared at the clouds outside. Was she offended by his offer or by the fact that his half-hearted apology for the hairy chest remark had not included her?

Although thirsty, I avoided alcohol of any type, not due to religious temperance but as it disagreed with me.

My companions resumed their solitary contemplations, the Reverend his bible, Mr O'Shane a game with cards and Mrs Drummond her knitting. It would be an exceedingly long and uninteresting trip.

Mrs Drummond was married and with child, although not to the point where hot water and clean blankets were required. Her skin was tanned and wrinkled already, surprising for a woman in her early thirties. I assumed her husband was a farmer as she had calloused hands from hard work on the land.

The Reverend in his black vestments was thin and with little hair. What he did possess was at the sides and back, his shiny pate covered with a broad-brimmed black hat. He sat opposite me.

As for Mr O'Shane, he was a mystery. I thought him a carpetbagger at first due to his strange bag, literally made of carpet pieces. The term was an American one I'd heard describing unscrupulous sorts who travelled the countryside, intent on exploiting opportunities for their own gain. Now, I was not as certain. He was a contradiction in every way possible if any person were to look past his banal exterior. Most of his language was that of the common man, a typical New South Welshman born and bred in our fine land. Yet occasionally he would let slip a word or phrase that suggested an upbringing by a family of means. He was of above-average education yet he chose to show it not. Why such a man would venture to this township of hundreds rather than thousands of residents, including the farms nearby, was beyond me.

My quiet musing as I half-dozed was interrupted by the guard next to the driver, leaning through the window to announce we should be stopping for lunch in less than two miles. It was a way-station for changing the horse. They were every ten miles or so, an innovation employed by Mr Freeman Cobb before he sold his enterprise.

We all welcomed the news. It was a chance to stretch our legs as well as partake of refreshment. The shotgun and driver would probably take turns as someone would need to remain with the coach and its precious cargo and mail. My worldly possessions were on the roof, as were the books I required in my new role as school ma'am.

Once we arrived, I held my breath as the cloud of dust that followed us caught up, shrouding the coach in a dusty, fawn fog. It would take me ages to clean myself after this trip was finished!

Being helped down from the coach by a gracious older man from the station, I surveyed our lunch accommodation. Mr Richie introduced himself as the way-station keeper along with his matronly wife then he hurried off to unhitch the exhausted team of horses from the traces and rig.

I moved to the shade of a coolabah tree by a river near the house. Mrs Richie joined me to offer a glass of refreshing lemonade. She'd already given the other members of our entourage theirs.

'It's beautiful,' I said, indicating the oasis of swaying trees that lined the small rapids and pool.

A flight of blue budgies, probably many hundreds, descended from the azure sky as one, to line the edge of the pool, each intent on sipping their fill.

'We enjoy it, Miss. Course it do get lonely at times but me and Mr Richie, we's got a good life.' Although we'd just met, she stuck me as a cheerful, winsome woman. The whinnying of twenty or so horses used to change the teams wasn't out of place. 'Lunch will be ready in a mo. Come inside and freshen up, Miss. The food's not up to your Big Smoke standards but there's plenty of it.'

The messenger shotgun came over to hand Mrs Richie several letters, tipping his hat to us. Mrs Richie beamed. 'From our son and his family in Wagga Wagga. Always brightens up my day. One of the advantages of being on the stagecoach route. That and getting our provisions delivered twice a day.'

Once inside the modest home, we washed up in the bowls provided then sat down as the station keepers fussed over us with more drinks including billy tea. The driver and shotgun joined us but not together as one stayed with the coach . . . just in case.

'Sorry about the rush on that last run, Miss Stevens. It'll be the same again for the next run, I'm afraid. I try to mix up the times we're on the road to confuse the bloody bushrangers. Excuse my language ladies, but them no-good, thieving bandicoots really rile me up, taking what's not theirs just like them highwaymen from the Mother Country.'

Mr Richie added his voice. 'Mad Charlie is the worst of them, by far, him and his gang. He's shot two constables. Didn't kill them, mind but they won't be the same men as they were. Life-changing injuries. Worse than death in some ways and the villain laughed as he shot them lying there defenceless. Laughed! He's a bad'un and there's no mistake.'

It was at that moment that I realised just how much like the wild west of the United States our Outback was. President Lincoln was assassinated scarcely twelve years hence and changes were happening here as well. The Colony of Victoria was formed from southern New South Wales and Queensland was taken from our northern parts. Even Van Diemen's Land was now named Tasmania. Was it any wonder that, amid all of the political turmoil of carving up New South Wales to form new colonies, the land was ripe for insurrection and chaos? The gold rush hadn't helped either for, as prospectors came to find their fortunes, so too do the vagabonds.

Mr Richie was called away to the stagecoach to aid in a minor repair. It was a problem with the throughbrace, the leather straps underneath the coach body that laughingly acted as shock-absorbers. I say laughingly as I was certain that the rainbow bruises on all our bodies bore testament to their questionable help.

At last, we were ready to proceed on our way. Although paid by the stagecoach firm to provide us with meals, I gave Mrs Richie some coin in appreciation of her gracious hospitality.

Then it was off again, further from civilization than I had ever gone before. Was I insane? I knew little of life away from Sydney Town and that spirit of adventure that had prompted me to embark on this painful journey was waning with every mile.

The road followed Billabong Creek

for much of the time. It made sense except where the waters meandered far from the direct between Narrandera and Jerilderie. As such we often passed through sparse woods of Acacia, Blackwoods and Eucalypts of various species. From my studies, they were nothing like the forests in mother England such as Sherwood where Robin Hood supposedly hid, in between robbing the rich. They were dense forests of oaks, elm and chestnuts with leaves of rich, dark green. Our continent of Terra Australis was much less blessed with life-giving waters and the trees adapted to such dryness. They flourished in their way, waxy coatings on the yellow-green leaves helping store water.

It was while travelling through one such forest that we felt the horses being reined to a sudden stop. I lurched forward, the Reverend bracing me from injury with hands on my upper arms.

'What's going on?' he called to the driver sat in front and above him.

I felt the brakes being applied and the

13

horses agitated.

'Tree across the road. Nothing to worry about.'

That was his reply. The coach rocked as the shotgun jumped down passing his weapon to the driver.

'Darn wattle trees . . . always falling down. They live for a few years, then that's it, especially after a storm.' Mr O'Shane was keen to reassure the ladies in the coach but I suspected his use of 'darn' might have offended our two travelling companions. Suddenly something fell onto the roof — or was it a fall?

There were words from above, the loud racket of a scuffle then I saw the shotgun land on the ground by my side of the couch. A lithe gentleman wearing a mask climbed down like a monkey, grabbing the weapon with his gloved hands.

'I believe it is customary to say 'Bail up' or 'Stand and deliver', ladies and gentleman. This is a hold-up. May I trouble you fine people to exit the coach, and coachman, will you please join them?'

Mrs Drummond gasped, her gloved

hand flying to her mouth.

'Best do as he says,' the Reverend suggested.

None of us was armed. I wondered about the shotgun messenger who had gone to shift the fallen tree. When we all stepped out to confront the bushranger, the answer was evident. He was being marched back to us at gunpoint by a second ruffian dressed in identical garments. They wore midnight blue trousers, shirts, masks and hats, the colour a parody of the police constables' tunics. Unlike the conventional kerchief worn by others of their vile ilk, these two had their heads completely shrouded by dark cloth with eye holes.

'Is this a masquerade ball or a joke, Mister? Why are you wearing that get-up?' It was Arthur O'Shane, reeking of drink from his hip flask. I suspected he'd drunk quite a bit at our lunch stop, enough for his mouth to open without him considering that these bushrangers with guns might not take too kindly to being insulted.

'A fair question, my good sir. I'm Major Midnight, a nom-de-plume to conceal my identity. I find it strange that my fellow bushrangers should blatantly advertise who they are, attracting the attention of all and sundry.'

'Major Midnight, eh?' Mr O'Shane persisted. 'What do you want, 'Major'?'

'Why to rob the Cobb and Co, coach and to show you and that pathetic company that no riches will be safe from me ever again. You, coach driver. Fetch me the money in that chest. Be quick about it or you'll be punished with a bellyful of your own buckshot.'

His accent, though muffled by his mask, was that of an Englishman, his demeanour professional and relaxed. This was no unplanned robbery and he was in no rush to be off.

'Do you want the mailbag too?' our suddenly helpful driver asked. The sight of the shotgun being waved around nonchalantly may have prompted his question.

Major Midnight gave a hearty, full-bellied laugh. He called to his masked accomplice. 'Did you hear that, Captain? Letters?' He faced the man on top of the coach who had dropped a heavy chest onto the dusty ground.

'What do I want with mail, my fine fellow? I have no interest in whether baby Billy lost a tooth or if Gladys Ponsonby is being married next month to a wheelwright in Outer-Coonabarabran. To steal letters between loved ones is simply unthinkable. They are not my enemies; the thieving bankers and owners of factories and coach lines are.'

Arthur breathed a sigh of relief. 'Does that mean that you don't intend to rob us? Not that I have anything of value, my friend, but I have noticed this lady has a very handsome watch in her purse. Silver, I do believe.'

I could not believe my ears! What business would it be for my travelling companion to mention my father's watch, given to me as a gift?

'A watch you say, my drunken reprobate? Thank you for the information. You

17

would do well to strike him, Miss, for betraying you. That said, I do need a fine watch. Perhaps I will make an exception to my rule about robbing passengers'

While his compatriot broke the flimsy lock on the strongbox to retrieve the contents, Major Midnight ambled up to me.

He was a tall man, five foot nine or ten and quite intimidating. Not seeing his features was unsettling. I tried to stay brave, only half-noticing the second thief taking the monies to put into four saddlebags from their horses. A gust of wind carried a stray banknote into the air but was ignored by the methodical accomplice.

'Your watch, Miss. Now.' I hesitated, trying to out-stare him. No way was I giving it to this gentleman thief. 'Miss. I have not yet shot a lady, especially one as fetchingly lovely as you yet there is always a first time. The watch, if you please.'

Acquiescing to his not-so-veiled threat, I retrieved my precious heirloom from my reticule bag. I passed it to him with a suppressed sob.

He examined it. 'To Grace, with all of my love. Are you, Grace?'

'Yes. It was a gift from my papa. I am surprised, Mister Bushranger. Usually, your sort are unable to count to ten on their fingers, let alone read.' I couldn't help myself, weapon or no weapon. He was a common thief, despite his protestations to the contrary.

'You certainly have a tongue on you, Grace. I pity your husband.'

'I . . . I don't have one, sir. If I did have, he would thrash you to within an inch of your dishonest life, I have no doubt.'

Although under the shade of the canopy of leaves overhead, it was uncomfortably warm. Everyone was fidgeting, impatient for this humiliation to be over. Yet the man before me and his masked companion were in no urgency to depart. In some ways, their brazen confidence was admirable. This Major fellow was unlike all the others who preyed on travellers. They would have been off long since but this man was an actor in a way, with us his audience.

'Relax, my precious Grace. I have no desire to take your prized timepiece from you. Take it back.' He pressed it into my open hand. Through our respective gloves, I felt him linger, his fingertips on my wrist sensing the rapid beat of my heart.

'However, I will steal another item from you in repayment of my gallantry.'

Faster than I thought possible, He grabbed my waist, pulled me to him and kissed me full on the lips! I was shocked, reacting far too slowly. He must have moved his mask as I felt the smooth stubble of his freshly shaven face as his lips pressed against mine.

Around me, I heard the others gasp. Such brazen effrontery, such rudeness! My eyes were open and for a moment I was staring into his eyes. They were steel grey. When he moved away, I took a deep breath as I had not breathed while he kissed me. How long had it lasted — mere seconds or a minute?

'Thank you, Grace. Your luscious

lips and the bank's monies are a grand reward for meeting this stagecoach this day. I hope my rash behaviour will not cause you further distress. We must now, as you say, make our getaway. You may have your shotgun back, old man. It will avail you not to stop us. Farewell, Grace . . . for the present.'

He bowed gallantly in my direction before mounting his steed, the saddlebags stuffed with monies from the strongbox. As for the shotgun, he tossed it into the undergrowth well away from the stagecoach.

'Remember my name well, my friends. Major Midnight. You'll be hearing of my exploits again, I wager. In years to come, you may tell your friends and relatives of the day we met.'

As they galloped off, the guard ran to retrieve his weapon, raising it to fire at the departing figures. Despite what had happened I wanted to cry out a warning, even if it would not be heard. I had no need to fear. The shotgun clicked noiselessly. The cartridges had been removed.

By the time others could be loaded, our assailants were motes upon the horizon.

Mrs Drummond came to comfort me. 'That brute, assaulting you like that! Are you all right, Miss Stevens?'

I licked my lips before answering. Mint . . . and something else? Parsley? 'I'm fine, Mrs Drummond. It was the shock of him doing that though it was, dare I say, gentle. And please call me, Grace.'

The older woman leant to whisper in my ear. 'Call me Matilda and please no jokes. My waltzing days are no longer. That kiss nevertheless . . . it brought back memories of my youth. I do believe our bushranger has a soft spot for you.'

She was more perceptive than I thought. I felt a warmth for him in my bosom, though I scarcely thought that Papa would approve. He'd known his share of ruffians yet wanted more for me, of that I was certain. As for the Major, he would be someone best visited in dreams rather than accompanying him to a dance or church. The mask might be too conspicuous!

The coach driver returned from somewhere, a box with cables in his hand. 'I climbed the telegraph pole to tell the authorities. No good. He must have cut the wires.' No doubt the coachman planned to call on the police for assistance using the Morse key in the box. The Major had foreseen the possibility and, like the attack, showed he was a planner who left nothing to chance.

We clambered back on board the coach, the fallen tree having been pushed to the side of the road. Our robbery drama was over. There was nothing more to be done but to head for Jerilderie and inform the relevant authorities. Life in the Outback promised to be anything than dull.

The team of horses were changed quickly at the next swing station. Our driver informed the stockmen there of what had transpired but they too could not get through on the telegraph.

We were fifteen minutes from there when, upon crossing a stream on a narrow bridge, three men appeared from under the structure to stop us.

'Bloody hell!' I heard the driver swear as he reined the team of horses to a halt. One of the masked men came up to us, the shotgun messenger tossing his gun into the water as directed. He was outgunned and he knew it.

'Bail up,' the masked leader shouted at the top of his voice. 'This is a robbery.'

2

'You lot inside, get out of there now.'
His voice was commanding, yet on the
squeaky side.

I opened the door seeing nothing but
water below me.

'Perhaps if you permitted the coach to
move off the bridge, it might be more
prudent,' the Reverend suggested, taking charge.

'Oh yeah. Right you are. Move the
coach forward and don't try nothing
funny, coachman.'

We rolled forward off the bridge
before disembarking on either side.
These robbers were also masked though
in a less fashionable fashion than the
Major. Already one of the thieves was
on the roof. He tossed down the mailbag as well as our respective trunks and
baggage. Mrs Drummond made a move
when her trunk burst open and her frilly
petticoats and undergarments spilt out

for all to behold.

A gunshot rang out as a puff of dirt exploded inches from her foot. 'Leave it be, Missus.'

'But —' she began to protest but I held her back.

'Do as he says, please, Mrs Drummond. He's edgy . . . and dangerous.' Whoever this bushranger was, he was ready to do something horrible at the least provocation. Mrs Drummond backed off, accepting the situation.

From atop the coach, the second man yelled out, 'It ain't here, boss.'

'What?' our captor exploded. Then pointing the weapon at our driver, he demanded to be told where the bank delivery was.

'He . . . he took it. Him . . . the other one.'

'Other one? Speak up, man. What other one?'

I offered to answer, 'The other bushranger. He stole it less than a half-hour since.'

I have never witnessed such a rage in a

26

man. He swore and thumped the coach with such ferocity that one of the painted panels splintered. I had little uncertainty that Mad Charlie Michaels was the man in question. After a minute of stamping back and forth, kicking stones and dust he managed to calm down enough to speak.

'That was my money. My money! I knew it was on there because I knows everything that goes on in these parts. I own this land. Me. And some no-good thief stole my money. He'll pay for that. By God and my right, he'll pay!'

It seemed a strange statement and attitude for one thief to be angry at another but I kept quiet for fear of riling this unstable person. Even his henchman dared not speak up when he was in such a foul temper.

'His name?' Charlie demanded, putting his gun against the Reverend's chest. I couldn't believe he'd do that to a man of the cloth. To his credit, Reverend Peabody didn't flinch, as he replied. Mad Charlie went into another childish tantrum before shouting, 'Major Midnight, eh? A strange name. A coward as well as a thief.'

The man on the roof tried to placate him. 'Not like you, eh, Mad Charlie?'

Immediately Charlie took aim and shot him in the arm causing his subordinate to tumble back onto the road. The third man scrambled to help his friend to stand, bringing him around to our side of the coach. It appeared to be a flesh wound as the chastened thief took off his kerchief and had it wrapped tightly over the bloody hole.

'How many times have I told you, Curly. Don't call me Mad Charlie. I ain't mad — just angry. Misunderstood. It ain't easy being a bushranger.'

'Sorry, Charlie. Didn't mean no offence,' the recently shot accomplice apologised, wincing at the pain from the wound. I couldn't believe him. Charlie must have been a hard taskmaster.

Introspection aside and realising he'd lost out on the bank money, the bushranger hefted the mailbag onto his saddle.

'Now you lot. Turn out your pockets and bags. I ain't leaving empty-handed.' Reluctantly I again did as he said, realising that my father's watch, so precious to me, would not escape his avarice.

They searched everyone but me and Mrs Drummond; in deference to our gender, I imagined. Our possessions were not as fortunate. Finally, satisfied they had all of value, they were ready to leave, but the good Reverend surprised us all by announcing that Arthur O'Shane was holding back. 'That gentleman is a gambler and a drunk. I saw him stash a wad of notes in his boot as we boarded the stagecoach in Narrandera. In so far as he told our previous robber of Miss Steven's watch, it is incumbent of me to return the favour. The right boot, I believe.'

If looks could kill, the Reverend would be standing at Saint Peter's gate very soon! As it was, Mr O'Shane's footwear was removed and the cash roll taken by Michaels.

'That was my stake money, that was, Reverend.' Mr O'Shane was not a happy man.

Michaels laughed. 'And now it's mine, gambler man. What a shame. You lot can go now, lucky that I let you live. As for this Major Midnight, he won't be as lucky when I gets my hands on him.'

The trio rode off soon afterwards, leaving me and Mrs Drummond to pack our muddy garments into our valises as best we could. It had been quite a day.

* * *

By the time we arrived in Jerilderie, it was late afternoon. We stopped outside the hotel while the two Cobb and Co employees hurried across to their offices and the police station respectively. That left the four of us passengers to retrieve our battered baggage. We were fortunate that the Reverend was adept at climbing onto the roof to pass down the luggage, such as it was.

Once I stood on the wooden footpath

with bags at my feet, I took a moment to survey my new home. It wasn't much; less than I had expected. This was a village that couldn't make up its mind, there being two distinct parts to it about two miles apart. I'd read that this split was down to two local men who each had their vision of where to make the town. To complicate it, a third had erected a general store opposite the Postal Office. Yet it was thriving from the sheep farms and prospectors frequenting this place for the drink, the commerce and, I hesitated to say, the presence of women to pass their time with on a purely commercial basis.

I should have been met by a representative of what passed as the town council yet there was no one around. Without guidance, I would have no choice but to find lodgings at the hotel, a prospect that filled me with trepidation. Also, I was hungry.

It was Matilda Drummond who noted my hesitancy to move. 'Are you awaiting someone, Miss Stevens?' I explained and she nodded sympathetically. 'People hereabouts don't pay much heed to the time as most don't have watches.' It was a thoughtless thing to say, given I'd had mine stolen, but she didn't notice. 'There are two places where a young woman might find a good meal and accommodation. The hotel is not for you. Might I suggest Ma Huxley's Boarding House? It would suit you to a tee. It's not far.'

'I . . . I haven't any money.' The few shillings I did have were stolen by Charlie.

'I'm positive that, given the situation, allowances will be made. No harm in asking, is there?'

'I suppose not. What about yourself, Mrs Drummond? Am I inconveniencing you on your return home?' Mrs Drummond was far kinder than I'd believed from our original conversation. I was quite taken with her.

'I live next door but one, it's on my way home.'

The walk was an education in itself. Jerilderie had character as did the people who lived here. That it was struggling to carve out a niche for itself in the middle of nowhere, was evident. Also, it wasn't far from the Murray River that formed the border between our colony and that of Victoria. Mrs Drummond spoke of increased riches for her town once the new bridge over the Murray was completed. Though there were times that riders could cross the almost dry river bed in places, for the greater part of the year the river was a barrier. Ferries from one side to the other were slow, cumbersome and expensive. More than one had been washed away to be dashed on the rocks, killing travellers and livestock alike.

I was introduced to a few of the townspeople but, my mind was not good with names. Today had been more distressing than I'd thought. By the time I lugged my baggage onto Ma Huxley's veranda and porch, the sun was casting a tangerine glow over everything. I rang the bell over the faded sign next to the screen door. I was in dire need of both food and a good wash.

Matilda waited by my side, keen to check that there was a vacancy. The door opened to reveal a smiling face — Ma Huxley I presumed. Her straw blonde hair was neatly arranged in a bun, her full figure showing a love for cakes and pastries. She was my idea of Mrs Father Christmas, a female version of that jolly old man so beloved by children.

'Matilda, you're back. And who is this charming companion you have brought with you?'

'Grace Stevens, ma'am,' I replied, warming immediately to her effusive greeting.

'The new schoolmarm,' Matilda added using an American term. 'She needs a place to stay, at least temporally. The problem is she has no monies. We were robbed on the Narrandera stage — twice.'

'I'm sure we can work something out, Matilda. Won't you please come in, Grace. And call me Ma. All of my guests do. Matilda? Are you coming in too? A cup of tea . . .?'

'No thanks. I'd best be getting back. I'll see you around, Miss Stevens. Good luck with your new job. Unfortunately, the menfolk who run things here might give you a hard time, 'especially Archie. I'm surprised he offered you the job.'

With a parting hug, she left as dusk was almost upon us and there were no gas street lights.

Ma Huxley helped me in with my bags, taking me through to a clean and comfortable room with a jug of water by a bowl for cleaning up. There were curtains and cushions, a woman's loving touch making me feel right at home.

'My other guests have already had their evening meal but I imagine that there's enough left in the pot to satisfy your appetite. Perhaps a slice of pumpkin pie, too. You need sustenance to put flesh on those bones of yours, heaven knows. Shall we say ten minutes?'

I thought of my pilfered watch but said nothing.

'Ten minutes, then. Thank you, Mrs Hu — Ma.'

My sleep was long and without interruption. When I awoke, I felt refreshed but quite sore from the punishing journey. The bed was luxurious and best of all, it was clean. The previous night's stay at Narrandera was a distant memory. I hoped that the disgusting insects in that bed had not chosen to accompany me. Deciding that there was no point in unpacking yet, I chose a pretty floral dress which was not soiled from being scattered near the bridge. To be robbed was one thing. To have my clothing and undergarments rifled through in public view was downright vile. I sincerely prayed that Charlie Michaels would be soon behind bars for his crimes.

That same feeling of detest did not extend to the other road agent, Major Midnight. My feelings for him were ... complicated. He was a bushranger, after all, but that stolen kiss ... I mused on it momentarily before readying myself for breakfast and

36

starting my new role as a teacher.

In addition to myself, there was one man dressed casually. From the state of his hands and general deportment, it was clear that he was no manual worker. I introduced myself as Ma busied herself bringing in our meals. Nothing had been said regarding payment for her hospitality and I was grateful that she didn't mention it in front of this person.

'Jesse. Jesse Travis,' the copper-haired gentleman said. His fair skin had freckles and had coloured by the harsh sun of these parts. I suspected that he was an incomer too and none too pleased to be in such challenging surroundings. A darkened office in Sydney's Pitt Street was more to his suiting.

'Ma said you'd come in by stage yesterday. Robbed too. It must have been traumatic for you, Miss Stevens.'

'It was,' I agreed. 'Not what I'd expected. I was recruited as the new teacher.'

He grinned. 'Pity you weren't my teacher when I was at school. You're a darn sight prettier than old Mr Vivian was. I felt the whack of his cane far too often, I'm afraid. Not the best behaved of students.'

I nibbled a piece of toast delicately before dabbing a napkin to my lips.

'But what do you do now, sir? The Black Stump is not your preferred location, I'll wager.'

It was an Australian expression. Those in the Outback were said to live the other side of the Black Stump. While Jerilderie wasn't quite that remote, I believed that the proverbial dead tree was not far distant away.

'Engineer, for my troubles. Charged with supervising the new bridge over the Murray.'

That was interesting. It was a long way to ride for a place to stay. I asked him about that.

He laughed. 'Oh, I don't stay every night. Maybe once a week for a bit of luxury, some decent food and to collect supplies from the store and blacksmith. He makes our ironwork. Usually, I'm in a tent with the team — along with tiger snakes, ants the size of your thumb and screeching cockatoos. I hate cockatoos. Reminds me of my ex-wife and her tirades.' He crossed his heart. 'May she rest in peace.'

'You didn't . . . ?'

'What . . . ? Kill her? No. An accident. Can't say I miss her.'

We ate in silence for several minutes.

Then I spoke up. ' Jesse? Isn't there some outlaw in the Americas with that name? Jesse Jones? No, James.'

'I believe there is. A robber of stage-coaches and banks. You are remarkably well-read, Miss Stevens. As for my name, we should not be judged by our appellations, or by our families. Would you not agree, Miss?'

I myself had had years of being the brunt of 'Grace, Grace, what a disgrace' while at school.

'Yes, sir. I do agree.'

He raised a china cup, regarding it with appreciation. I imagined he was used to a tin cup of billy tea, barely as enjoyable.

'Besides, Miss Stevens. Being named Jesse does not make me an outlaw. Stare closely, do I resemble a bushranger?'

It was my turn to laugh. 'Hardly, sir. Yet they do wear masks to conceal their features.'

He turned his gaze to the bread, freshly baked from its aroma. I watched him. The way he moved. There was a familiarity about him in some way. I thought of the Major. No. Impossible. The Major was two to three inches taller and a good stone heavier than this slightly built gentleman.

We chatted more but the time came for us both to be on our ways. I was to see Archie Applegate, the leader of the town Progress Association. He ran the local brick kiln and had plans to expand the bakery and small flour mill he also owned.

Ma Huxley, who was dressed in a colourful frock and apron, told me there would be a meeting of the Association at 9.30 at the mill on Powell Street. The Creek was behind.

Fortunately, my credentials and books had not been taken by Charlie although they had been scattered around the site of the hold-up. I packed those certificates that I had into my reticule bag and set off. It wasn't that far to walk and the unexpected cool night had chilled the morning air. I kept to the shade, for the greater part, arriving at the mill in good time. They were expecting me, I hoped, as I had written to confirm the offer of my appointment and my proposed arrival date. I knocked politely on the door marked 'Office', hearing the animated chatter of men laughing as they discussed business. There was a woman's voice too.

'Come on in,' someone called and I entered.

'How may we help you, Miss?' the man sitting behind a large mahogany desk asked. He must have been Mr Applegate, a man in his mid-thirties with greying black hair. Although a businessman, he was a man who didn't shy away from physical work. His broad shoulders showed that.

'Hello everyone. I'm the new teacher, Grace Stevens. Pleased to meet you.'

You could have heard the proverbial pin drop as the four men and older woman stared at me and then at one another. Finally, Mr Applegate stood, taking the cigar from the ashtray to puff it.

'That can't be right. You're a woman.'

This was becoming a worry but I decided to press on. 'Last time I looked. yes. And let me guess. You're a . . . what's the word? Ah yes, you are a . . . man?'

One of the other men, a portly bloke of advancing years spoke up. 'Miss Stevens. It's nothing against you. Please have a seat.' He indicated a vacant armchair.

'I'm the local banker, Mr MacTavish. What I believe Mr Applegate was trying to express was . . . well, this is a growing township and as such, it can be rough. We have bushrangers and shootings, hardly the type of environment for a woman of refinement such as yourself.'

Archie Applegate wasn't quite as diplomatic. 'Miss Stevens. There has been a dreadful mistake. Even though our most influential member Mr Younger is not present, I believe he would agree too. Your services are no longer required. I suggest you get the noon stage today.'

3

Archie Applegate wasn't quite as diplomatic,' Miss Steward. There has been a

Flabbergasted, I stood there, hands on
hips feeling as angry as I had when bailed
up yesterday. To be robbed was one thing
yet to be cast aside for my womanhood
was so infuriating. I would not stand for
it.

'Mr Applegate. I have spent five days
travelling to this township for a position
that you offered me. Five bloody days in
a bone-rattling death trap surrounded
by drunks and stinking individuals of
all persuasions. Furthermore, there
was yesterday's attack by two — count
them! — two separate gangs of bushrangers. You have the gall to dismiss me with
a wave of your hand. How dare you, sir!
I have no monies to buy a return ticket
or to pay Ma Huxley for her hospitality.
I insist that you reconsider. This instant.'

My cheeks were flushed with anger and
Archie Applegate wasn't accustomed to
being addressed like that — let alone by

a person of the female persuasion. The entourage turned to Archie to gauge his reaction. He sat staring at me, somewhat taken aback.

The banker spoke up. 'Perhaps we can compensate Miss Stevens for her trouble?'

'What with?' the woman said. 'A new bushranger stole the cash shipment. Bad enough that we have one of the thieving scroats, now it's open season for Jerilderie. Pretty soon there'll be advertisements in the Wagga Wagga Courier, telling every bushranger in every colony to head here.' The others nodded.

What had I landed myself in? I had arrived expecting a steady wage for my services. Maybe I should accept my losses and return home to Papa, my tail between my legs.

'I can pay,' Archie announced. 'It was my mistake. I mean, what woman in her right mind would accept a teaching position here? I just assumed you were a man.'

'But my application stated my name.

Surely that gave you a clue as to my gender?'

'My fault . . . I don't . . . I don't read very good. That's why I wanted our children to get an education. But not with you. As I said, no place for a woman . . . well, a woman such as you. We need someone strong who knows how to cope.' He had recovered from his maudlin state and was adamant that I should leave.

However, I wasn't prepared to. His confession about his literacy problems and desire to improve the lot of the local people had decided me. It was time to make him change his mind.

'As I told you, Mr Applegate. I may appear to be a delicate lady, ready to run and squeal at the sight of a mouse but things are not what they might seem to be. How about you and me decide if I can survive in this township of yours in the traditional way of you men . . . a boxing match to decide if it's the best man or woman that is triumphant.'

There. I'd thrown down the gauntlet.

There were cries from all present, save from the woman. She instead gave me a nod and a wry smile.

'That would be out of the question, Miss. Uncouth and rough might we be, yet Mr Applegate is a gent and to strike a woman . . . ? It's unthinkable.' It was the banker who spoke loudest. Mr Younger would certainly object if he were not busy elsewhere.

It was my turn. 'I said nothing about striking me — simply that he is welcome to try. I warn you, I will not pull my punches and would expect no less from you, sir. What is it to be? A fight, here and now? Or sir, are you as yellow as the wheat used in this mill?'

The owner stood, hands gripping the desk. Even so, there was no anger there. 'Goad me not with your jibes, Miss Stevens. I have never raised a hand to a woman and despite your challenge, I see no need now. Make your way back to Sydney Town if you wish. I shall pay your expenses.'

'Ah, a coward then. Perhaps you need

further prompting, sir.' I took the cotton glove from one hand and, in a move that caught all unawares, slapped him across his ruddy cheek!

'The fight, Mr Applegate. I demand satisfaction!' I gritted my teeth. I was going to stay and be accepted as an equal if not superior to these men.

He touched the stinging skin. 'Very well, Miss Stevens. You have your fight. I must protest as to your wishing to do so. It is most unbecoming.'

'Think of it as a bushranger who hides behind a mask one moment then pretends to be a model citizen when the mask is removed. I am a lady but I can be someone else as well. Today, I choose to be your opponent. The Marquess of Queensberry Rules will guide us. No punches below the belt.'

Chairs and tables were pushed to the walls as space was cleared. The woman aided me to remove my remaining glove, hitch up my skirt and fasten my wavy hair back.

'I'm the owner of the hotel, Miss

Stevens. Try to be compassionate in this fight. Mr Applegate is a proud man yet good in his heart. He loves this tiny town.'

'You realise who I am?'

'I believe so. I used to admire your father, a hero to many a young woman. I suspect he taught you well. It's not too late to tell them. Mr Applegate will let you stay.'

'No,' I said. 'A point needs to be made. I am my father's daughter. This is the only way.'

'As you wish. Good luck.'

I unclenched my fist. 'There is no luck save the one we make for ourselves. Would you help unbutton these boots?'

At last, we were ready, squaring off one another. We shook hands. I chose to squeeze his giving him a hint of my strength. He was surprised though tried not to show it.

His advantage was strength, mine my nimble feet and years of training. He didn't have a chance. His first swing was tentative, without conviction. I dodged

49

it, delivering a blow to his chest. He staggered back, surprise in his eyes. His next strike was angrier but easy to dodge as I danced from one foot to the other, avoiding other attacks each time.

The score was five telling jabs by me and none by him when I decided to end it quickly with an uppercut to his jaw. That floored him. He lay sprawled out on the planks, rubbing his injured chin and grinning.

'Enough, Miss Stevens. You've made your point. Welcome to Jerilderie.'

I reached out to help him stand.

'You lead with your right, Mr Applegate. Fatal. Perhaps I might give you pointers for your future bouts.'

No one could believe what had happened, save the Hotel proprietress.

'Shall you tell them about yourself, or should I?' she asked me.

I was still catching my breath. I was a little out of condition. 'You, Mrs.'

'Gentlemen. Meet Grace Stevens, the daughter of Daniel Stevens.'

It was Archie Applegate who twigged

the connection first among the men.

'Dynamite Dan Stevens? Well, blow me down! No wonder you did me in, Miss Stevens. I gave it all I had at the end but you . . . you were playing with me. I don't feel as bad now. It was a pleasure to be decked by you, Miss — although my jaw might not agree.'

He came to shake my hand, with genuine friendship this time, as did the others.

I'd found my role in this town — at least for the immediate future.

★ ★ ★

There was talk of our colony of New South Wales making it compulsory for all children to attend schools. There were insufficient trained teachers or schools built to allow that commendable dream to happen, even in the larger outback towns. To have a small place such as Jerilderie, choose to set up their school was a testament to the progressive nature of Mr Applegate and the others here.

I'd been selected as a pupil-teacher at the age of fourteen and gradually trained so that now, at the age of nineteen, I was qualified to teach without supervision. The usual class size was fifty or more children of all ages. It had been challenging but I'd coped.

The gathering accepted my youth as fine for a teacher, explaining that once the school was established, an inspector would visit to accredit me and the school. They would then change the present method of one half my salary being paid by the Progress Association and half by our fair colony to full payment by the government. They would also build a suitable school house at their expense.

'You will be using our School of Arts hall for your school, Miss Stevens. We do use it for other purposes such as our monthly dance which attracts landowners and workers from miles around,' said Archie, insisting I call him such. 'You should find a suitable husband in no time as there are many men to choose from. Jerilderie has a paucity of women as you may have noted.'

'I assume there is no such shortage in the Hotel, sir.'

Archie blushed. 'Itinerants, who generally stay at the hotel. Men have their needs yet a woman of refinement such as you, Miss Stevens, would not understand.'

'Call me Grace, please. And I'm not as innocent of the ways of men as you might think. My father had a reputation with the women of Sydney Town. He still has.'

We were making our promenade to the village hall to inspect it and the school materials and furniture gradually acquired over the past months. My teaching would commence on Monday giving me and the children five days to prepare. There would be but a dozen boys and girls to start with, more expected. Their ages would be five to fourteen.

'Your father is a widower, I gather, Grace.'

'Yes. My mother died of consumption when I was but five.' Tuberculosis was a dreadful disease that ravaged her poor body. There was no cure. 'My father had many friends and between them, they ensured my education in both the three 'r's as well as social graces and others of a more physical nature.'

Archie rubbed his jaw, before giving a warm greeting to a group of men and women gathered on the main street.

'By physical, I assume you mean boxing?'

'Among other pursuits. My skills in embroidery and sewing are not as well developed. I am, to use the vernacular, a tomboy in disguise.'

Talking of disguises, I was again reminded of my close encounters with those two bushranger gangs. I had mixed feelings as the Major had been very gallant and chivalrous to me. The silken touch of his lips upon mine had stirred emotions that I'd repressed as best I could. No plans for marriage, home-keeping or the raising of half a dozen children for me. Although I was chosen by the Lord to be a woman, I regarded myself as good as any man. But I knew the prejudices that persisted in this male-dominated world. It mattered not that the Empire was ruled by Queen Victoria, men were in charge and were reticent to lose even one iota of that power.

'These bushrangers, Archie?' I asked as he indicated that we should turn down a side road to the hall. 'Tell me about them, please.'

I could sense an immediate change in his mien, sorrow shrouding his answer.

'They're parasites, sucking the life-blood of our community. People are becoming afeared of travelling to and from this town for being robbed, or worse. Even Cobb and Co are reconsidering the viability of sending coaches. Without that lifeline for our mail, money and provisions, as well as passengers, the town will wither as an English rose in the drought of summer.'

'They sever the telegraph to disrupt communications, and rob the coaches with impunity, secure in the knowledge they will not be caught. You've driven through on the coach. There are hundreds of square miles of wilderness, hills, ravines. They can hide anywhere and strike at any time. We have two policemen. Two. And they aren't paid enough to search everywhere. The sole consolation is that they have not brought their thieving ways into our town.'

'They knew of the bank shipment — both of them.' I recalled that fact.

'Spies, informants. Michaels has friends, some in high places. I wish I could find out who. Our last Reverend apparently heard one of them in a conversation with Charlie's gang. He was shot soon afterwards to make certain he told no one who it was. Even a woman, such as you, could be murdered if you ask the wrong questions. It's one thing to win a boxing match with an old bloke like me, quite another when three or four men confront you with guns.'

We'd reached the School of Arts hall and the following half an hour was spent on the mundane realities of my new role.

Archie gave me monies in advance so that I could pay my way with Ma Huxley. He also suggested that I ask for a permanent arrangement with her, the only other accommodation for single women being at the hotel. Hearing what happened there on a nightly basis, I had to agree with him.

I was given a position with the Progress Association too. School teachers were often assigned that task due to their standing, therefore I accepted that.

Once he left me with the keys, I settled down to hard graft, aware that I was wearing my best frock. Cleaning and the heavy work could wait for another day.

All in all, it was a rewarding morning. I'd return to Ma Huxley's for lunch as arranged and perhaps take a stroll around the town this arvo, as well as the creek behind Powell Street. It was as I passed the hotel, that I noticed two riders coming up the street.

Where do I recognise you from, mate? I wondered. It was the clothing, right down to the grey kangaroo skin hat. He glanced my way momentarily. The reason that I did not know his face was that it had been hidden the last time I saw him. It was Charlie Michaels, brazenly trotting along the street as if he were an ordinary citizen! Well, mister bushranger, I'd see about that!

Parasol in hand, I hastened along to the town police station and pushed the door ajar. In the dark, coolness of the room, I waited for my eyes to adjust.

'Can we help you, Miss?' There were two offices seated on the other side of the counter, cards in hand. Their kepi caps were on a hat stand, their blue woollen tunics unbuttoned and their white breeches were not clean. In short, they were a slovenly pair. The one without the pipe in his mouth had asked the question.

'Yes, thank you, officer. Charlie Michaels just rode into town. He's over there.' I pointed through the dusty window at the rider, now dismounted and not twenty yards distant. 'He stole my watch yesterday and robbed the stagecoach.'

58

They failed to budge, giving me an indifferent once over. 'What makes you think this bloke is a bushranger, Miss?'

This was unfathomable. 'Why? He's Mad Charlie Michaels.'

One of them, at last, stood to come towards me. 'That's Charlie Michaels right enough but he don't take kindly to being called Mad. We know him a-passing-like and he's no criminal. He's nothing to do with the fellow who robbed the stagecoach. I saw him here in the hotel, the time of the robbery.'

'But several people have told me what he does and yesterday one of his henchmen called out his name as the stage was robbed. We all heard it.'

The policeman was condescending as well as lying. 'Miss. Anyone can use another person's name. I could call meself Prince Albert. Don't mean I'd be him.'

'Particularly as he died of typhoid goin' on twenty years since,' the seated constable added. They both chortled, showing great disrespect to our Queen's

59

great love and consort.

'But it was him. He's even got the boldfaced cheek to wear the same clothing as the man we saw yesterday.' As with Archie Applegate, I was under the impression that a woman's opinion was to be ignored in this male-dominated town.

'Could you identify his face, this bushranger from yesterday, Miss? If you can then we could act, assuming the rider yonder has the same face as this bushranger bloke.'

'Of course, I can't do that. The thief was wearing a mask, a kerchief over his face.'

The standing officer sat back again, lifting his cards. 'Then there's nothing we can do, Miss. You see we police needs proof. Sorry.' They recommenced their game of poker.

'What sort of place is this?' I shouted but received no answer. It was evident that any further demands for justice would be ignored. I turned to leave when the door flew open and a very dusty, exhausted gentleman came in. It was the engineer from the boarding house, Jesse Travis. He staggered to a chair and asked for water.

'Mr Travis,' I asked. 'Whatever is the matter? I thought you were taking those supplies back to your camp.'

'I was, Miss Stevens,' he gasped before calling out to the police. 'Officers. I wish to report a robbery by that bushranger.'

'Which one? There are two gangs around this area.' I inquired expecting him to say Charlie.

'Don't think so. There were two of them. One called himself Major someone or other. He was with another called The Captain.'

I couldn't believe it. 'Major Midnight?'

'Yes. That's his name. Evil creature. He shot the new man I had with me. Gunned him down in cold blood.'

'And . . . ?' one constable asked.

'Then he threatened to ruin every business and bank in the area.

4

I had to ask. 'Jesse? Mr Travis? Where's the man he shot?'

Jesse looked devastated. He was covered in dust and sweat. 'Dead. Those bushrangers threw him on the wagon before riding off. I was left stranded — no horse, no nothing. Took me a good three hours to walk back here. I'm well and truly bushed.'

'Who shot him, your new man?' I was trying to take this all in. The Major and his partner were thieves but surely not murderers.

'One who called himself the Major. He was calm while he did it. Execution style. All Peter was doing was riding with me to help with the bridge. Bloody thing was, he wasn't even . . . even armed.' He wiped the back of his hand across his eyes, fighting back his emotions.

'Why take the body, Mr Travis?' The older policeman must have known the engineer from frequent visits for supplies and fresh workers he recruited from the drifters always coming through in search of work.

'One reason. no proof of murder. Just my word for it. I reckoned that out while walking back.'

There was a lengthy silence . . . a gloom had settled upon the four of us much darker than the night. Murder was murder. Next to bank robbery and horse stealing, it was something unimaginable.

One of the troopers spoke. 'Get down to the Telegraph office, Herman. Mr Travis? We need a description of the wagon and horse he stole.'

Jesse gave them a run-down including the stolen provisions, mainly food, drink and metal braces for the bridge structure. He also named the young victim and described him. He'd met him riding into town as Jesse was leaving so none of the townsfolk had seen him.

'And his horse?' asked the constable.

'Sorry . . . horse?'

'This bloke . . . Peter? He had a horse

hitched to your wagon I suppose if yous two were on the seat.' The constable was noting this all down.

'Oh . . . oh yes. A bay. Didn't take much notice, I'm afraid, being from the Big Smoke and all.'

I cast a questioning glance at him. It seemed to me he'd been caught out by the question.

Once finished, he said he'd go to the Telegraph office to send a message to his base of operations on the Murray River. He'd need another rig for a fresh set of supplies. As we left the station, I said goodbye to Jesse, although it wouldn't be for long. He said he'd be coming back to Ma's for lunch with me and staying again tonight. There were no other boarders at the present. As we left, I overheard the police making plans to investigate the scene of the crime with Jesse later. Then I caught a half-whispered statement between them. 'Better tell the boss. He won't be happy. This Midnight bloke'll screw up everything.'

Ma Huxley was overjoyed that I'd secured my new position and would be staying with her for the foreseeable. She was even happier once I paid for last night and the following two weeks in advance at our agreed rate. I imagined a regular boarder was preferable to the hit-and-miss of passing travellers.

She kindly offered books from her grown-up children plus crayons and other items to use at the school if I wished. It was a generous gesture.

Naturally, I told her the news of Mr Travis's misfortune and the murder. It was difficult to accept that the man who had kissed me so tenderly was the same one who had committed such an atrocity. Was Mr Travis mistaken? After all, as the police might have said, any man could completely cover his head, dress in midnight blue and pretend to be whomsoever he chose. Jesse did seem adamant that the thief was the real one.

Yet what if he made up the story for a

nefarious reason, to steal the goods and blame it on a convenient scapegoat? I chose to ask Ma what she knew of Jesse Travis . . . I mean really knew.

'He's been coming regularly once or twice a week since late July. Always has those drawings with him, detailed engineering plans to the bridge. Seen him working on them most nights in the parlour and doing sums and ordering materials. Two weeks ago, he brought experts on the construction site to help sort out problems anchoring the bridge. Charming men, especially Seb someone or other. I've met him back in Bathurst. Small world, I guess. Seb's shy but quite a conversationalist when he's relaxed. He'd worked with my late husband when we lived in Bathurst and I do recall Cyril mentioning him as a friend.'

Ma paused at the mention of her late husband's name, lost in memories of their time together. At that time, there was a knock on the front door. Expecting it was Jesse Travis, I offered to answer it as Ma was lifting cakes from the oven.

Jesse looked terrible, desolate at the loss of this Peter bloke in addition to the supplies and wagon. He had a word with Ma, before going to clean up. There was splattered blood on his shirt, so Ma offered to loan him some of Cyril's while she washed and dried his. Having no luggage or cash to pay her, she made light of it.

'Those bushrangers will be my ruin. All those penniless victims coming into town and me being a soft touch, giving 'em free beds and supper.'

No one laughed, although Jesse did promise to make good once Seb Longstreet arrived with a replacement wagon and team of horses this arvo.

'Seb Longstreet. That's the bloke I was telling you about, Grace. I'm surprised you're taking him off the job with the bridge, Mr Travis?'

'Most of the team are professionals and there's a brilliant foreman overseeing it all.' Jesse laughed. 'There are times I wonder what they need me for, apart from the fetching and carrying.' Then his face became sombre again; the thought of what had happened to him this morning perhaps. There was so much drama happening in my adopted home town and these rival bushrangers were at the heart of it all.

Jesse appeared after several minutes, clean and in different clothing. After prompting, he passed his bloodied clothes to Ma who took them away. The three of us settled down to our meal, but we were interrupted by a rap on the entrance. I went to answer, surprised to welcome the Reverend.

'I came to see the man from the bridge-building team, Miss Stevens. Pastoral guidance. I believe he stays here?'

I invited him in. 'This is the Reverend Peabody. He came with me on the stagecoach and wishes to see Mr Travis. You both have had the same misfortune to meet with that scoundrel, Midnight.' There must have been a vehemence to my tone that surprised the Reverend.

'Miss Stevens. I'm puzzled. If I recall that 'scoundrel' kissed you yesterday and you did not object. If I might be so bold you actually liked it!'

The other two stared at me. I blushed. 'That was yesterday. Today I have discovered he killed a man and robbed poor Mr Travis in broad daylight. Quite frankly, this Major is not the gentleman he purported to be.'

There. I'd said it. Whatever had possessed my youthful nature to be smitten by this criminal had vanished like dew in the morning sun. I listened as the Reverend explained he'd come to offer spiritual solace to Mr Travis if he wished. When Jesse said he'd welcome time alone with the man of God, Ma Huxley suggested that he join the three of us for our light lunch then he and Jesse could have privacy.

We had a meal of bread, salad and cold wongawonga pigeon in a bread sauce. The Reverend said grace then we tucked in. He was looking forward to us attending services on Sunday.

After finishing our meal, the two men excused themselves as we tidied the dishes away. I told Ma I was heading to Billabong Creek and the lake at the back of the town. The School of Arts (my school) backed onto the creek and I wondered if we might leave the confines of the classroom to enjoy the benefits of nature at times. It might have been regarded as a distraction by other teachers but I was not conventional.

Ma offered to accompany me, suggesting it might be a suitable occasion to meet a few of my future charges as they often fished, played or swam in the creek around this time of day.

We left the gentlemen. Jesse would be accompanying the officers to the scene of the robbery and murder then returning to meet with the employee bringing the replacement wagon for reprovisioning the construction team.

It was a warm September day, a gentle zephyr of air stirring the air into willy-willies that picked up dust, swirled it around then dissipated as though they were never there. We had our parasols to protect us from the harsh sun but the bulky dresses we women were expected to wear caused further problems. Ma had a basket with her to collect some goods from the shop.

For a small town, the streets were busy with solitary horses and riders as well as wagons and drays. Pedestrian townsfolk waved to or greeted us showing the strong sense of community. We passed the church, a modest affair with a sign giving service times for those who could read and a hand-painted notice saying that the church was open again.

'It's down this way, Grace. There's some trees right by the waters and Mr Applegate had two seats built under them to afford shade for those residents who enjoy a break. They can watch the creek gurgling by.'

Away from the relative clatter of wheels and hooves, the melodic sounds of the birds and sheep bleating gave an air of tranquillity to the scene before us. Then there came the lullaby tones of the waters flowing over rocks before reaching a tranquil lake with ducks and swans performing their meandering explorations.

'Why, this is lovely,' I commented with a smile.

'There's an unspoken rule hereabouts. No shooting of the animals near or in the town boundaries. If anyone fancies rabbit or kangaroo steamer, there's enough close by.' Kangaroo steamer was an Aussie version of an English delicacy, jugged hare.

Both the bench seats were empty although two older boys were fishing well away from us. Four boys and two girls were playing games too.

We brushed aside leaves and other garbage from the weathered wood and sat to contemplate the view before us. Flies buzzed by us as did butterflies, and beetles as large as my thumb. After a few minutes of relaxing silence, Ma chose to ask me about myself.

In truth, there wasn't much to tell. I had no illusions to understanding the so-called mysteries of life let alone people. My father, despite what I had said regarding him being worldly, was always very cosseting and protective. We were well off without being rich and I'd been fortunate to have the intelligence as well as opportunity to learn far more of the world than my contemporaries. I'd read widely, my favourite authors being Mr Charles Dickens and the American, Mark Twain. Marcus Clarke's *For the Term of his Natural Life* about convicts in Tasmania's Port Arthur showed the talents of my fellow countrymen. It had been published three years ago.

Ma was quite a follower of boxing so was impressed that my dad was Dynamite Stevens. Once she told me that she'd been married yet had no children, I was a little puzzled. She explained that she ran an orphanage in Bathurst but, following Pa's death, she'd moved on.

'Why Jerilderie?' I asked.

'Why not? Sometimes we go places and do things that are not logical, as well you know. The Fates are fickle and unravel the threads of our lives in intricate ways. I came here four years ago and found a fresh family to be a part of. It was fine until the bushrangers arrived. Now I feel that it's not just precious metals and cash they have stolen from this place; they have taken that spirit of hope and togetherness that first attracted me. What's worse, there's a danger of Jerilderie becoming a no-go area and that won't be good for my trade.'

I nodded, staring absentmindedly at the rippling reflections in the pond. 'There is another thing that's worrying you, though, more than the bushrangers?' I said, turning to stare deep into her dark brown eyes.

She moved her gaze to the hands clasped in her lap. 'My goodness. You're a perceptive girl, aren't you?' Then she looked all around as though she was afraid to be overheard. The children were far off and the only creature nearby was a wallaby grazing not fifteen feet from us. Her next words were in a whisper, spoken close to my ear.

'Bushrangers are one thing. You can see them coming, masks disguising their faces. It's the other ones, the men pretending to be respectable but with their wicked agenda to bleed our town dry. Don't ask me who they are as I do not have proof, only suspicions. I hear things, snippets of conversations and phrases which may be nonsense but they are there, nevertheless. No cotton masks for them, save a smile or a handshake to make you believe they are your friend. If I were you, Grace, I'd keep my own counsel. Trust no one.'

'Except you,' I suggested.

'No. Not even me. People have their secrets and that includes me. Watch your back, Grace Stevens . . . for both our sakes.'

★ ★ ★

We discussed happier things as we watched the children playing. Then another boy appeared and seemed to summon his companions. It was hard to hear over the creek and birds but it was a rhythmic chant. Soon, the others joined in repeating the garbled words. It might have been a new nursery rhyme or a poem; children loved repetition and learning a few lines to repeat them to others was a fine teaching tool.

'I wonder what that's about?' I mused.

'Why not find out. I'll introduce you to your students, Grace, then I must be off to the shops to stock up for our meals. Come on. Just help me up, will you? Getting old.'

The girls and boys came to us as we approached.

Ma introduced them by name. I struggled to remember names and faces but did my best.

'This is Miss Stevens. Your teacher. She'll be starting on Monday.'

The children were all excited apart from one girl who told me that her dad didn't approve of girls learning the three Rs, especially as she had her chores to do. When I told her that I'd see if I might change his mind, her eyes lit up. Emily was no more than six.

They had all sorts of questions so I sat

with them on the lush grass to try and answer. Ma Huxley took her leave with a smile.

'My Dad says after I's go to school. I'll be able to read books and stuff, Miss. Is he right?'

'Of course, he is, Billy. Reading, writing, 'rithmetic. The three 'rs'. You'll learn them all.' He was around eleven. 'First thing we'll do is teach you to write your name.'

Then I recalled that chant I'd heard earlier, requesting them to repeat it for me. They all joined in, enthusiastically . . .

The Cobb and Co coach to Jerilderie flew,
'Bail Up! Bail up!' said the man in dark blue.
'I'll have your cash or there be a fight
Beware my name, Major Midnight.'
A mask on his face to cover it well,
No one seen it 'cause the dead they don't tell.
Troopers can't find him, he hides far from sight
Bushranger most famous is our Major

I was surprised rather than shocked. Out of the mouths of babes . . .

'Goodness. This Major Midnight sounds scary. As a matter of interest, where did you learn this?'

'Henry told us,' Billy explained, pointing to an eight-year-old.

'And who taught you, Henry?'

He was reluctant to answer. 'At the pub, Miss. My mum works there . . . behind the bar,' he hastened to add. 'That new bloke Mr O'Shane was telling some other blokes at the card table. Did I do summat wrong, Miss?'

Not that I disapproved. It was simply a rhyme.

'Of course not, Henry. But why are you interested in this Major Midnight? He killed a man this morning, you all realise?'

That brought sadness to their eyes but it was little Emma who spoke up first.

'People get shot in our town, Miss. Reverend Carstairs, he was killed. He was a good man who used to tell us stories in

Sunday School. He was funny. We all miss him. But Major Midnight . . . he might be bad, but he's famous. Mr O'Shane told my daddy that he used to be in Tasmania but he shifted to here because the troopers there were making things too un . . . uncom . . . fortable for him and The Captain. He showed Henry Wanted posters and read it to him.'

This was a little bizarre. Arthur O'Shane of all people. Why would he be carrying Wanted posters? Was he a bounty hunter? Stranger still that he'd not said anything regarding the Major on the coach or when we'd been robbed by him.

Billy must have realised the connection between me and the gambler. 'Fair cow, Miss. Oh — begging your pardon, Miss Stevens. My dad's a bullock driver and I picked up bad words. I try to be more what me mum wants but you know, it slips out at times.'

I'd heard my share of colonial oaths from the larrikins in Sydney and wasn't easily offended but a woman, especially a teacher, had to maintain standards.

'You are excused, Billy, but only this once. Now please go on with what you were saying.'

He was still excited. 'You and that Mr O'Shane. You was on the stagecoach that was robbed, yesterday. You saw the Major, didn't you?'

I nodded.

'What was he like, Miss?' an older girl asked but I'd forgotten her name. I was probably six years her senior. She wore dungarees and had short hair.

I ignored my initial surge of blood to my cheeks to focus on the events rather than my feelings. There was no possibility I'd tell them he'd kissed me. 'Well, my first impression was that he was a gentleman. He was British and polite. His mask covered his head except for his eyes. He didn't have a beard. When I heard of the shooting it was a total surprise. What did the Wanted poster from Tasmania say?'

They turned to Henry. He shrugged his shoulders. 'Can't read, Miss.' Then he grinned. His dirty hands searched through the pockets of his torn clothing, eventually extracting a folded piece of paper.

'I didn't steal it from Mr O'Shane, Miss. Just borrowed it, like.' He handed it to me asking me to read it to the group.

'I will, but you must return this, Henry. It's wrong to steal. It's one of the Ten Commandments. And borrowing without asking is stealing.'

He stared at his muddied feet, suitably chastised.

After opening it, I straightened the creased poster. There was an artist sketch of the bushranger in masks and hat. I read out, 'Wanted. Dead or Alive. Major Midnight. Murder and robbery. £1,000.' Underneath in small print were the crimes he was guilty of. They were extensive, a veritable litany of crimes. The document was authorised by the Government of Tasmania. No wonder he'd fled Tasmania. At the same time, I wondered about extradition to another colony. If he'd fled to Victoria, I suspected he could not be arrested there unless he committed a misdeed in that colony. That he was wanted in both New South Wales and Tasmania would not matter a jot. And Victoria was less than a few hours ride from here.

'Is that a lot of money, Miss?'

'Yes, it is. But enough of that, children. I believe it's time for us to head home.' The sun was low in the afternoon sky and other animals were making their way to the Creek. There was a fat, old wombat wobbling along.

'Hooroo, Miss,' the children chorused.

'Hooroo. And Henry, please don't forget to return that poster.'

'Yes, Miss.'

I dusted the grass and twigs from my dress and set off back to Ma Huxley's. What a first day it had been!

★ ★ ★

Jesse immediately stood as I entered the parlour of the boarding house, out of deference to my gender. His companion didn't but I felt his gaze as he appraised

82

me like a prize ram through his tinted glasses.

'Miss Grace Stevens? Seb Longstreet.'

I reached out to shake his hand but was ignored. How uncouth, I thought, noting his slovenly nature and dirty skin. He should have washed up on his arrival at this cosy and clean establishment. At least he'd only be here for a single night.

'Seb?' said Jesse, uncomfortable with the situation. 'Miss Stevens is the new teacher.

'G'day, Teach,' he muttered at last. His light brown hair was short yet unkempt and he was without a beard or moustache. His demeanour was that of a typical colonial male, the sort who thought women were good for one thing. He must have sensed the contempt I felt for him as he sat up. 'What you staring at, lady — my dirty clothes? I can take them off for you but I reckon it'd be better somewhere more private.' Then he laughed.

I could feel my skin crawl. 'In your dreams, Mr Longstreet,' I replied vehemently, before realising that wasn't the best comeback.

'You're right of course. You're far too skinny and that wavy blonde hair of yours looks too similar to a sheep's fleece for my liking. Anyways, I suppose we gotta put up with you for a few days at least.'

'A few days . . . ?' I felt suddenly nauseous.

Jesse spoke up, apologetically. 'Er, Seb's right. We have to stay over until Monday. The blacksmith can't finish the replacement engineering parts until then.'

Absolutely great! Four nights sharing my accommodation with Jesse wasn't a problem but his pet pig as well? Then I recalled Ma's comments about him. We obviously had differing opinions regarding blokes.

There was a frantic knock on the front door. Being closest and wanting to get away from Seb, I opened the door. Henry was there sobbing. I ushered him in. He noticed the two men and tried to wipe his eyes, being reluctant to speak in front of them, I guessed.

'These are my friends, Henry.' I smiled. 'Well, one of them is, at least. What's the problem?'

'I'm sorry, Miss. He took the poster I was giving back to Mr O'Shane. I couldn't stop him.'

The men exchanged glances.

I knelt in front of Henry, brushing his hair back and wiping his teary eyes. 'Start at the beginning, Henry. Who took it?'

'Him. Mr Michaels. Snatched it from my hands, he did. He was awful angry when he saw it.'

'The beginning, Henry,' I coaxed, trying to calm him. Seb and Jesse had come over to listen.

'Well, I was walking up Powell Street, singing that Major Midnight poem when he stopped me. Then he saw the poster and he started cussing something awful, Miss.' His eyes were darting between the men and me.

Seb knelt by my side, taking his glasses off. 'It's all right, son. The bad man's gone. Perhaps if you say this poem? Mr Travis here and I would love to hear it,

85

wouldn't we, Mr Travis?'

Seb's face was inches from my own as we both knelt near the boy. Instantly, he had Henry's trust. I couldn't believe it, certainly not from the man I'd recently met. His voice was soft, the strong Aussie accent not so pronounced. The man's entire mien had become more caring.

Hesitantly at first, then with more confidence, Henry repeated the words about the mysterious Major Midnight.

Seb and Jesse gave him a little clap and that brought a smile to his face. By this time, Ma had entered to see what the fuss was all about. She gave Henry a freshly baked biscuit and that made him happier still. As he nibbled it, savouring every bite, I reassured him that I would explain what happened to Mr O'Shane's 'borrowed' poster and for Henry not to worry. Seb tousled Henry's hair then faced me before standing and adjusting his dark glasses. Henry left, still with that biscuit in hand. It was getting dark.

'Mr Longstreet. What you did to reassure Henry was very commendable. I might have misjudged you.' This was a genuine attempt to mend bridges.

'No worries, teach. The kid reminded me of my brother, that's all. As for me, lady. What you see is what you get. Like it or lump it.'

'Perhaps, Mr Longstreet. Perhaps.' I had suspected that Seb Longstreet had secrets of his own and that brash exterior was not the real person. The first question was why should he have this facade of arrogance around me — and should I be concerned enough to care?

I had the distinct sensation that I'd met Mr Longstreet before. It would come to me in time.

5

I changed into another frock for the evening meal and was in the kitchen helping Ma. At the same time, I chose to unpack my baggage. Those that were clean were packed into the veneered walnut wardrobe and the highboy drawers, the soiled clothing needed a good scrub. A piece of paper fell from one dress as I unfolded it.

It was a crisp new ten-pound note. Papa must have slipped it into my bag at home as I'd left. I popped it into a drawer. Tomorrow, I'd send him a telegram to thank him for his heartfelt gesture.

As there was a mirror on the wall, I tried to sort out my hair, tying two light blue ribbons near my ears after brushing the unruly curls into a semblance of tidiness. At least errant strands wouldn't be tumbling over my face as I ate. I dabbed some lavender water behind my ears, took a deep breath and went to the dining area. Time to face my fellow guests.

Whatever was cooking smelt great. Ma Huxley was grateful for my offered help. The 'boys' were nowhere to be seen. Typical men.

'I gather that you and Seb didn't hit it off too well this arvo, Grace,' she said casually as I carried plates and other items through to the cosy adjoining dining room. There were four guest bedrooms and scarce enough room for eight people in the unlikely event it was fully booked.

'Cat and dog would sum it up, Ma. Talk about rude. Didn't seem to respect your furniture either. You told me your husband knew him in Bathurst? If that's the case, you and he must have had the patience of a saint.'

She grinned. 'Seb is . . . well, let's say, changeable. He's a dark horse is that one, but underneath that gruff exterior, he has a heart of gold. Give him a chance and you'd be surprised.'

I was sceptical. 'A heart of gold, eh?

From what I've seen, Major Midnight or Mad Charlie must have stolen it then.' From the sideways glance that Ma made, I realised I'd opened my big mouth at precisely the wrong moment. Seb and Jesse strode into the room, although Seb was grinning at the remark rather than scowling.

'Look at us, Miss Stevens. We've met a few hours ago yet we're fighting like a married couple. No wonder, I find you . . . endearing. For that reason, I reckon I'll take you to the dance Saturday evening.'

I sputtered at the arrogance of this man! He certainly wasn't shy as Ma had described him. Perhaps he'd matured like stinky cheese that had been left too long. Yet he did appear quite presentable, hair neatly combed and his tanned skin damp from a recent scrub-up. His clothes accentuated his muscular build. Rather than the creature I'd met not two hours since, he gave me pause for thought. That was until the clumsy oaf tripped and fell, steadying his ungainly

90

body barely in time to avoid knocking me over too.

'If your dancing is as good, I should be wise to decline your presumptive offer. Besides, did your mother never advise you that it is more polite to ask a woman than to treat her as property at your beck and call? I cannot go with you. Mr Travis has already kindly asked me and I accepted.'

Jesse hadn't done any such thing yet it was the first excuse I came up with.

'You sly old dingo,' Seb laughed, slapping him on the back. 'Then it looks like you and me, Ma. If that's all right with you.'

I declare Ma went red as a beetroot! 'Why yes, that's lovely, young man. It's been a while since anyone asked me.'

We settled down to a nutritious meal of a fish called Callop or Murray Perch. Seb had caught it on the way into Jerilderie, therefore it was fresh.

'I reckoned on catching a Murray Cod,' he explained. 'As big as a shark. I got one last week at the camp. Five-foot long and I'm not exaggerating. Took three of us to land it.'

We were all enjoying the food and drink. Seb was sitting opposite me and our gazes kept meeting, try as I might to look anywhere but at him. I delicately cut some potato and choko before eating it. 'Jesse told me he hates roughing it down at the camp,' I said then checked with Jesse to see his response.

'Seb knows how I feel regarding the bush. I detest it. Trouble is, I have to go where the work takes me and this bridge is the biggest job I've done. That's why we need all the ironwork to make the joints secure. Seb's the bushman, not me.' He gave a chuckle, recalling an incident. 'Last week he had to save me from wild pigs. He reckoned they thought I was one of their own because our hair was the same colour.'

It was strange, Jesse being jovial after his brush with death not nine hours earlier. I had to mention it. 'For a man who's seen a companion killed by that Major Midnight, you don't seem too upset, Jesse.'

The smiles and laughter faded. He stared at me then Seb before replying, having put his knife and fork on the plate. 'Maybe that's how it seems to you, Miss, being from the city. I was similar to you a few months ago. Coming out here was a big adventure. That attitude changed when a friend I made was murdered by that Mad Charlie bloke. Of course, no one can prove it was him what done it, but the townsfolk know. I realised that you have to accept that people get shot here. That's why I'm not too upset by that Paul fellow this morning got himself killed.'

'I thought his name was Peter?' I questioned.

'Peter . . . Paul. It doesn't matter. He's dead, rest his soul. I'd met the man an hour earlier, offered him work then he gets himself shot by arguing with an armed robber. A waste of life. He'll never have a Christian funeral. As for those troopers who came with me to the crime scene, they were useless. We tried to trace where the bushrangers drove off in my wagon but that Major, he was too clever by half. Drove over rocky ground so no wheel or hoof tracks. Their hideaway could be anywhere.'

I felt there was a reluctance to discuss this, and I turned my attention to Seb as he'd become quiet. 'What do you reckon of this Major Midnight, Mr Longstreet? Do you have an opinion or don't you care what happens around Jerilderie?'

'I care, Miss Stevens. More than you imagine. One day in the town and you're passing judgement on law-abiding citizens. I've not met any bushrangers, nor do I wish to. I certainly haven't kissed one.'

I bristled with anger but restrained my response. 'The Major forced himself on me, sir. Like Mr Travis this morning, I was helpless. The man had a gun for goodness' sake.'

How had Seb found out what had happened? No one but the three passengers and the Cobb and Co people had seen it and, to my knowledge, Seb had arrived from the Murray without speaking to them.

He thumped the table with his open hand, grinning like the cat who'd eaten the cream. 'Ah-hah! So the rumours were true. Did you hear that? Kissed by Major Midnight, hisself. Was he a good smoocher, Miss Stevens, this bushranger who you let kiss you? On a scale of one to ten, was he soppy as kissing this fish or did he stir the passions and make a pretty woman's heart flutter with lu-u-rve?' His relentless teasing was more embarrassing to my companions than me.

'Have a care, Seb. Can you not see that it was a distressing experience for the girl?' Jesse had risen to my defence.

'It was a zero, my vicarious Mr Longstreet. I've had more passion from a soggy lettuce than the Major. Perhaps it would be better to change his sobriquet to Major Disappointment, methinks?'

Jesse burst out laughing, but Seb said nothing.

When the moment had passed, I needed to explain my concerns. 'To be honest, Mr Travis, The incident this morn with the Major seems at odds to the behaviour of that bushranger we met. Any Tom, Dick or . . . or Seb is able to wrap a blue scarf around his features and claim to be Major Midnight. The troopers suggested that Mad Charlie Michaels the bushranger was not the same man as Charlie Michaels the man I saw in the street today, even though he did wear the same garments. If I wished, I dare say I can wear blue and call myself Major Midnight.'

I sat back pleased with the point I made. The gentlemens' eyes stared at my figure and shook their heads.

'That may be stretching the imagination too far, Miss Stevens. Your high-pitched voice and . . . other things would betray your gender, scarf or not. Tell us, what do you know of this bushranger?'

I sat forward, my plate clean but for bones. 'He is from Van Diemen's land, now called Tasmania. I saw a Wanted poster from there. Also, the children have learnt a poem about the scoundrel. Mad Charlie saw and heard them and was most displeased according to one of the boys. I'll wager there is room for but one bushranger in Jerilderie and Charlie intends it to be him.'

The men exchanged surreptitious glances as Seb polished his spectacles. What were they thinking? Claiming the reward? I doubted it. It was more a flicker of excitement, the look of anticipation of two boys waiting for a rabbit to spring a trap as they watched from afar. When they returned their attention to me, I arched my eyebrows and smiled one of those unnatural smiles that wedded couples did for a photographer. I did not doubt that Seb Longstreet and Mr Jesse Travis were anything but the labourer and engineer they purported to be. Big schoolboys showing off their skills at repartee in front of a young woman — me. They were from two different worlds yet had a familiarity of long-time friends, working together on various engineering tasks, I imagined. Each was comfortable in their respective world but had formed a school-chum bond where they didn't need to establish a pecking order so common when two men met. It was a comfortable relationship where each trusted and relied on the other.

I envied them that. My friendships with girls were shallow and transitory. My desire to have a best friend had never materialised and I regretted that deeply. Being raised without a mother might have contributed to that but as my father always maintained, there was no point in crying over spilt beer. The past was the past and that was that.

* * *

A sing-along after the meal was very enjoyable although it had been hard to read the music in the candlelight.

Seb's tenor contrasted well with Jesse's unusually deep bass voice. We sang *The Wild Colonial Boy*, *Moreton Bay* and several other bush ballads with varying degrees of agreement on the lyrics. *The Wild Colonial Boy* was an old favourite telling us of an Irish lad, transported to New South Wales and becoming a bushranger. He was shot by another Irishman, a trooper called Fitzroy. It was based on a real outlaw according to Jesse. Glorifying the life of a bushranger in song reminded me of the Midnight poem.

Whether it was our convict origins as a colony or an innate anti-English streak caused by the intense heat, a rebellion wasn't far from the minds of the poor wanting a better life. New South Wales and the other newly formed colonies were searching for their identity. We were halfway around the world in a country with bizarre animals and plants, and some people were desperate to break free from the apron strings of Mother England. And if bushrangers became Australia's modern-day Robin Hoods, I reckoned to understand the reasons. Admittedly, I wasn't enraptured with that thieving scoundrel Mad Charlie for taking my money and my watch but as for the Major and the mixed feelings I had for him ... Darn. Why wasn't life easy?

* * *

The first point of call was the Telegraph office to send a telegram to Papa, letting him hear that I'd arrived safely and to thank him for the hidden money. It wasn't too warm when I left, therefore I thought I'd visit Arthur O'Shane, to discuss that poster situation. I doubted that he'd be too concerned at its loss.

Henry ran to me as I bravely entered through the swing doors. I'd seen my share of hotel interiors yet was a little concerned that, in this town of double standards, a woman in a pub was frowned upon.

I was introduced to the barmaid, his mother. There was no one else there but she suggested that Mr O'Shane would be down from his room soon. In the meantime, she thanked me for coming to help with the education of the children and explained that I would always be welcome.

'If a lazy, good-for-nothing bloke objects, he's gonna get bloody thirsty, bloody quick. We're the sole pub in town and what I say goes, if you catch my drift.'

At that moment, there was a commotion outside. We all looked through the plate-glass window at the two constables riding at full gallop to the south of the town.

'Wonder what that was all about?' I mused, surprised to see them doing anything, let alone with such vigour.

'Probably off to get their bribe money,' was my companion's quiet explanation. As if realising she'd have muttered too much, she resumed polishing glasses behind the bar.

I decided to take a seat at one of the tables but had second thoughts when I saw the state of them. It was lucky that I didn't need to.

'Speak of the Devil. Or should I say Sleeping Beauty?' the barmaid said before calling out in a shrill voice to someone descending the stairs, 'You have a visitor, Mr O'Shane.'

He came over to take my hand and kiss it. A whiff of cheap whisky and an even cheaper woman's perfume helped hide the other, less agreeable odours. 'Miss Stevens, as I live and breathe. Am I that irresistible that you would come to me at cock crow in the morn?'

'Hardly, sir. I recall that I almost lost my watch because of your loose tongue . . .'

'But all that happened was a kiss by that Midnight fellow. Am I to blame for that too, hmm?'

I felt that I was Eve standing under the apple tree in a discussion with a serpent. They would have shared a lot, especially the monotonous sleazy tone plus the lisp. It would surprise me not to find out that Mr O'Shane's tongue would be forked like Lucifer's.

It was time to get to the point but the

gambler was more intent on the pocket watch he had somehow replaced. Mad Charlie had taken his, as well.

'You have a poster of Major Midnight from Tassie, sir?'

'Not 'have', Miss Stevens. 'Had'. The barmaid's urchin took it and gave it to some ruffian, I gather. It is of no consequence. It is not as though I could claim that reward, each colony's laws being what they are.'

'Then why have it? Do you expect to meet him on the coach and ask for an autograph?'

He stroked his moustache then his saggy chin before removing that damn watch from his waistcoat. Another glance to the street then faced me. I noted he was sweating. A soiled kerchief was produced to mop his brow.

'Of course not. I use the backs of scrap paper for reckoning on though it be none of your business, Miss. If you'll excuse me, I can hear the tinkle of a glass with my breakfast in it. I think it best you leave bef —'

He stopped his explanation as gun-shots were heard echoing through the streets.

'Get down!' I yelled to the others, instinctively. Mr O'Shane didn't budge. His attention was on the road outside. I pushed him down then I peeked from my flimsy cover behind an upturned table. What was he staring at? The street was suddenly empty, horses tied to hitching posts outside the Cobb and Co offices across the street.

Another shot. Louder this time.

Two figures in blue appeared from the inside of the stagecoach building, fired into the air to dissuade all would-be heroes, then mounted the steeds effort-lessly. Midnight chose to do a trick rider stunt as the horse was already galloping off.

They were gone in an instant, notably in the opposite direction to where the police had galloped earlier.

'Bloody hell!' the barmaid gasped, slowly budging from her protective refuge behind the bar front. 'That was Midnight and his Captain. Bloody brazen! Broad daylight in the middle of town. What if the troopers had been here?'

I had the answer to that. 'I reckon the police had a tip-off that Midnight was spotted south of town. That's why they left in such a hurry. That allowed the bushrangers to come in from the north and escape the same way. Wonder what they stole? Have you any idea, Mr O'Shane?'

The gambler was dusting his clothing off from being pushed to safety on the floor. His moustache looked a little worse for wear too. He glowered at me, 'Me? How would I? I was here the entire time.'

There was no point in pressing the matter. He'd expected that robbery. It was the reason for his disquiet, staring out the window and his watch.

By this time concerned citizens were milling around the uninjured official from the Cobb and Co office. I joined them outside in the sun, eager to hear what had transpired. Archie Applegate arrived, breathless. He'd come at the noise of gunfire.

'Horatio, what happened?' he asked the greyhaired man in uniform.

The older man was shaken and the words tumbled out from his mouth. 'That Midnight bloke. He — he was there in the office, bold as brass. Told me what he wanted. Said no one'd be hurt if I gived it him. S — sorry, Mr Applegate. Awful sorry. He had a gun.'

'Sorry? What f...? Oh, dear Lord! He took it, didn't he?' Archie Applegate collapsed to the street, his skin as pale as a new-shorn sheep. Someone went to fetch water.

It was the banker whose name escaped me resumed the interrogation. 'The gunshots, Horatio. Did he try to kill you like that drifter yesterday?'

'No, Mr MacTavish, sir. Fired through the roof. I gived him what he asked for, quick smart. Cobb and Co don't pay me enough to end up in the cemetery. He took the package and disappeared fast as a possum up a gum tree. Even thanked me and apologised for putting holes in my roof.'

'And you were sure it was Major Midnight?' the female hotel owner checked.

'Fair dinkum. Spoke his name in that Pommie voice of his and introduced that Captain fellow, polite as anything. Didn't take anything else, just that package to Wagga Wagga what you gived me, Mr Applegate, as if he knew it were there.'

'Archie,' said the rotund banker bloke. 'What was in the package?'

Archie staggered to his feet with help from townsfolk. He looked as sick as a dead chook. 'Don't matter now. It's gone and that's the end of it. The sole consolation is that he doesn't suspect where I found it.'

I chose not to add to Archie's worries but if there was some valuable object there and Archie knew where there was more to be found, the businessman's life was in danger from Midnight.

Questions filled my head though, like several pieces of a complex jigsaw but without a painting to see how they connected. How did Midnight learn of the mysterious package? Was it the same way that he was aware of the bank money on our stage? Mad Charlie wanted that cash too so they both must have had inside information as it was not common practice to advertise movements of bank-notes. This township appeared replete with mystery and intrigue, a veritable real-life novel.

My goodness. What had I got myself into? Four robberies in three days and one of them in the heart of Jerilderie. It was the lawless wild west of the United States right here in our Australian colony! I turned to leave as the doctor had arrived to tend to Mr Applegate and Horatio but the old official from the Cobb and Co offices noticed me.

'Excuse me, lady. You're the new school teacher, aren't you? Miss Stevens?'

I felt conspicuous as all eyes were upon me.

'Yes, I am sir. Grace Stevens. Why is it that you enquire?'

'I remember that Major Midnight told

me a message to pass on to you, should I see you.'

This was very perplexing and further raised the hairs on the back of my neck. 'Go on please, Horatio. Though I know not what such a criminal would say to me. I met him once on the Narrandera stage. It was not a pleasant experience being assaulted at gunpoint.'

Horatio hesitated, realising that we both had an audience. I decided to press him. What would he possibly say to embarrass me?

'He . . . he told me that . . . he wishes you a good day and that your hair . . . well, it's as shiny as the golden sun.'

6

I see you.'

Although it was not of my making, I felt
ashamed for the rest of the day. It wasn't
logical yet I did. It was one thing to have
wolf-whistles from lads on street cor-
ners, but to have the inference that I was
romantically attached to a bushranger
was quite wrong.

I beavered away at preparing the village hall for the lessons that would start
on Monday, scrubbing and cleaning to
the point where my fingers were red raw
and every muscle screamed in protest.
From behind me on my hands and knees,
I heard Matilda Drummond exclaim.

'My goodness, girl, there's no need to
be doing all this! All you needed to do
was ask for help.'

I stood up slowly perspiring from the
effort and the fire in the hearth, boiling
water for the buckets. 'Matilda. Good to
see you. What time is it?'

'Nigh on two, Grace. Have you had

lunch?'

'No. Not yet.' I sat on a bench at the furthest point from the fire in a coolish breeze coming through a door. Matilda sat by me as I patted the adjoining seat.

'Perfect. I have sandwiches and fresh lemonade. You deserve a break, my girl. Ma Huxley won't be long and some other ladies are coming to lend a hand. We might not be a big community but we stick together, the womenfolk least-wise.'

There was a pump inside the hall, probably connected to the creek running behind the hall. I went to wash my hands and face ready for the sandwiches.

'We all heard what happened with young Horatio this morning.' I gathered it was one of those local expressions as young Horatio was one of the oldest people I'd seen in town. He was probably a stagecoach driver, too worn out to control the teams any longer.

'Oh,' I replied before we both took a chunk out of the doorstep sarnies.

'I cannot work out how that

smooth-talking Major learnt of Archie's special dispatch. Neither can Archie. He kept it a secret, 'cepting for Horatio. He's devastated.' Matilda clearly knew him better than I.

'What was in it?' I wondered.

'Won't say. I gather he discovered precious stones or metal and was sending it for verification. Now that Major Midnight has it, he'll want to find out the location. Archie doesn't have a clue. He was sending it for someone else he says.'

I thought for a moment. 'Sounds very cloak and dagger to me. Hidden treasure goes with Long John Silver and treasure maps.'

I could understand the secrecy. Jerilderie might suffer the same fate as Bendigo and Ballarat did twenty years ago. Wherever gold was found, such as with Orange in our colony or the Adelaide Hills, prosperity followed, along with an influx of prospectors. Without careful management, the chaos of the first few months there could strike Jerilderie too, causing a lot of damage.

Archie had attempted to keep it low key, but if Midnight had the samples then he wanted whatever riches there were for himself and himself alone.

'Wasn't there gold found in Tasmania? Major Midnight was there. Bushrangers follow prospectors just as flies follow sheep.' Except, in this case, it seemed that Midnight planned to by-pass the middle man and snatch the riches from the very lands they had lain undiscovered for so long.

* * *

During the afternoon, several other residents called in to lend a hand or supply books or materials to help establish the school. A few men arrived with a large blackboard and boxes of both white and coloured chalks. They expertly fitted it to the wall which I indicated.

'Courtesy of Frau Schneider, Miss Stevens. Reckon you and the little'uns can use it more than her,' a polite worker explained.

'Frau Schneider?' I asked Matilda.

'You met her that first day. Runs the hotel. Hard as nails but has a soft spot for the kiddies.'

'Oh,' I said, puzzled why a hotel would have needed a blackboard. I addressed one bloke. 'Please, thank her very much for me.'

'I will, ma'am.' He put the hammer and other tools away, prior to mentioning how excited his daughter was at learning to read. I told him to call me Grace. He gave me his and his little girl's names. Conscious of my sieve of a memory, I wrote them in a book I kept in my apron.

'Is that my name?' the gentlemen said, trying to trace his huge fingers over the letters.

Sensing genuine wonder, I led him to the blackboard and wrote David Smith in capitals then bit by bit guided him to write it underneath. I took my time with him, sounding each letter as I guided him to copy my efforts.

We didn't notice we had an audience until he finished, his face beaming with the broadest smile I'd ever seen. The letters were wobbly but they were there. There was genuine praise and clapping.

'I wrote my name,' he announced, his eyes misted over. 'Can I try again?'

'Of course. Try the coloured chalk too.'

I'd only taught children but adults might be interested in learning too.

I printed David's name on a leaf of paper and gave him a pencil to practise his newfound skills whenever possible. I'd seen the shame of grown men and women who, when asked to sign their name, managed to make their mark with an X. This ability to write and read, even a little, was life-changing and was the right of everybody, child and adult. I sincerely prayed that the future of all the colonies of our continent would be inexorably linked with education to allow our citizens to achieve their innate potential.

As I bade him good afternoon out the rear of the hall, I noticed Archie discussing things with Jesse. They were a good two hundred yards off wandering through the undergrowth on the other side of the lake area. What on earth would those two have in common? I did not realise they were acquainted with one another. Seeing me, they waved, resuming their deliberations which now included the creek.

A telegram boy arrived on a bicycle with a message for me. Assuming it was from my father, I popped it into my pinny to read later. There was still a lot to be done in the hall.

It was gratifying to find this many people, both male and female, ready to lend a hand. I made a note of each of their names with a brief physical description for my benefit. All I needed was a prompt to remind me.

As the last couple left, I gathered up my possessions and took one final sigh of satisfaction at the result. I was ready to depart when Archie arrived with a few small blackboards for the pupils to do sums on.

'Looking splendid, Miss Stevens. Congratulations.'

'I had a great deal of help, Mr Applegate.'

'As I was certain you would. Jerilderie is a fine community. If only we can tame the criminal roughnecks and bushrangers like Charlie Michaels.'

'Don't forget Major Midnight. He stole your goods this morning.'

Archie said nothing to that which was surprising. Nor did he elaborate on what had been stolen. He had his reasons and it wasn't my business to question that.

'You are coming to the dance tomorrow evening? We start early to permit those who prefer to depart in the light. Unlike Sydney Town, we have no gas lights on the street and even with the full moon, it's difficult to drive or walk home.'

'Oh, my goodness. The dance . . .'

The look of horror on my features must have worried him a lot as he gently put his hand on my shoulder. All of our hard work would be undone and I'd have to redo it on Sunday afternoon to prepare the school for Monday's lessons.

'Don't despair Grace. We have a team of volunteers who will set the hall up for the social on Saturday but more importantly restore it, ready for your lessons. You've done your bit but if you wish to oversee everything, you will be welcome. There's a storeroom next to the kitchen. The school materials can be stored there tomorrow and brought out on Sunday. There's no need to panic. We want you to enjoy your first dance in Jerilderie.'

We closed up and began to walk towards the main street. The sun was a huge pink-tinged globe slowly disappearing on the horizon and the birds were searching for their places to nest overnight. The crickets had begun their night-time chorus joining in with frogs in the bulrushes to provide a noisy if not melodic farewell to the day.

'By the way. What were you and Jesse discussing?'

'It's a bit hush-hush. I was interested in his views of putting two bridges over Billabong Creek. It would cut five miles off the journey to the Victorian border.

The Creek winds around a lot south of here and it's a waste to have to follow it on the road. It won't be cheap but it should benefit the town.

One of the troopers almost bumped into us as we turned the corner. He was in a rush. It was dark enough that I was unable to choose who it was. They were the same height with scruffy jet-black hair and handle-bar moustaches. Recalling one of my favourite books while growing up, *Alice Through the Looking Glass*, I was minded of Tweedledee and Tweedledum. I'd brought it with me, to read to the children. It was perfect for stirring their imaginations to write their own adventures then read them to the class.

'Miss Stevens. Glad I found you,' said Tweedledum. 'I wanted to ask you to the social tomorrow night.'

I tried to be genuinely apologetic. 'Oh no, Constable. You should have asked me earlier. Mr Travis has already invited me and I accepted. Such a shame.'

He stared back at me, mouth agape in

a fine impersonation of a fish gulping for air on a riverbank. The resemblance was upsetting.

'Is that a no. Miss Stevens? I really had my heart set on it and if you want a recommendation, Maisy Jane at the hotel says I'm a bonza bloke.'

'It's a no, Constable. But please do thank Maisy Jane for recommending you.' At that moment he was neither of Lewis Carroll's imaginary characters. He was a brand new one; Tweedledummer!

The constable was preparing to slink away into the shadows but Archie had other ideas.

'Constable Younger. Any news on my package from this morning? Bad enough you head off because of an anonymous tip-off, allowing Midnight to rob the office bold as brass. Surely you have an idea where he's hiding?'

'No dramas, Mr Applegate, sir. We reckon we know where he is.' He paused for dramatic effect. 'Out there somewhere.' He waved his hands all around proudly. 'But rest assured, he ain't within coo-ee of town right now, not with me and Herman keeping an eye out for the bugger.'

Archie rolled his eyes at me. 'Thank you for your insight, Constable. I feel much safer with you and your older brother on the job. As a matter of interest, how do you find your boots when you wake up in the morning?'

I smirked yet concealed it behind my hand. Sarcasm was lost on this law-officer.

As if to prove my point Constable Younger responded with a toothy smile. 'I just looks down the end of my feet in bed and there they are, snug as a bug on my little feeties.' He tipped his peaked cap to me, then took his leave. 'Hooroo.'

We waited until he was out of earshot before bursting into laughter.

'He's as much use as false teeth made of soap, him and his brother, but we can't fire them. Politics. Their father is a big landowner nearby.'

Archie did warn me about getting

too involved with Jesse though. 'He is a fine engineer but, even if he does build our bridges, he won't stay for long.' He waved farewell then we made our separate ways home.

Dusk had almost fallen. I needed to catch up with my diary tonight. So much had happened. As for the telegram, I'd completely forgotten it was there in my apron.

★ ★ ★

Almost a day later and it was time for the highlight of Jerilderie's social calendar, the monthly get together. It was a chance to put on your Sunday best, brush your hair and, in the case of women, put on their blush and rosewater. I tended to avoid lipstick and eye-liner made from lamp soot as my father pointed out that it was the preference of ladies of the night. Also, being slim-waisted, I preferred not to be suffocated in a corset or wear those impossible bustles that accentuated my derrière.

I was not a typical woman. Fortunately, Australian women were less constrained by the vagaries of fashion than those in Mother England. Even in Sydney itself, women were more independent and less inclined to strangle our bodies so that a man could compliment us on our slim waists. I'd heard of women passing out because their corset restricted their breathing too much. Cutting the offending stays to split the garment had saved more than one lady's life as she lay prostrate on the floor. I'd seen advertisements in the Sydney Morning Herald promising a waist of 20 inches. Whether that was achieved by tightlacing from an early age to train the body shape or by removal of the floating ribs at the base of the rib-cage, neither was for me.

Jesse presented me with a corsage to wear. Where he'd found it, I had no idea. As we departed for the hall, however, I noticed a similarity between my flowers and those in Ma Huxley's carefully tended flower bed.

Seb was wearing the same clothing

he'd worn on his arrival but it did appear (and smell) cleaner. He complimented me in a typical back-hand way. 'You look mighty pretty, Miss Stevens. For a girl.'

'I'm nineteen, Mr Longstreet. My teddy bear days are in the past. There's many a female of my age married and with children. Don't suppose you've ever found anyone desperate enough to marry you, though?'

'The evening's not yet begun, Grace. Mayhap I shall find my Cinderella here before the clocks strike midnight?' Whether it was the way he turned away as he said Midnight or the self-conscious way he removed his glasses without gazing at me, I was intrigued.

'As a matter of interest, why wear dark glasses, Seb. Do you not want to be recognised?'

'What? A nobody such as me? No, the glasses are to protect my eyes from the sun. A problem when I was a child. It's called photo-sensitivity. Makes me trip over things at times as I can't see too well but at least I can manage. I'm not too keen on lights either. Not a very manly thing to admit but my skin has thickened over too many taunts at being a coward. These days and with this build, I'm lucky that people mistakenly believe I can take care of myself.'

It was a strange admission of vulnerability from a man who was a contradiction in so many ways. Also, his friendship with Jesse. They were poles apart and it was difficult for me to accept their friendship.

'Where are Jesse and Ma? I thought they were right behind us? You don't think . . . ?' I asked, choosing to lighten the mood.

He laughed at that. At that moment they appeared, each laden with bags of food that Ma had been busy preparing. 'A sort of welcome party for you,' she confessed.

Jesse was much better dressed than his male working friend, surprising as he purportedly lost everything in the robbery of his wagon a few days earlier. I asked him about that as we set off arm in arm.

'As I stay in Ma Huxley's once a week, I leave a bag there with my better clothes in it. Some may call me a peacock for my love of fine clothes yet I do not care. I am a creature of habit and even finding myself at the back of Woop Woop, will not alter that.' To illustrate his point, he touched the bow-tie he wore. 'Pure Italian silk. A touch of luxury to remind me of the grander things in life. I do miss the theatres and shows of Sydney. Can't wait to get back there.'

I sensed his homesickness. 'And yet you are in discussions with Archie?'

He seemed puzzled then nodded. 'Ah yes, the bridge.'

'Two bridges, you mean? To bypass the meandering river?'

'The same bridge design in two places. Engineer speak. As I said earlier, I must go where the work takes me. Until I am famous and my talents allow me to pick and choose. I have a dream, you realise. To be the designer of a magnificent metal giant that spans the Sydney Harbour from the south side to the north. A huge arch of steel supporting road, pedestrian paths, a tramway and railway.'

'That would transform the city. I'm impressed, Mr Travis.' I snuggled up closer to him after planting a peck upon his cheek.

Behind me, I heard an 'Oh la la,' from Ma Huxley. I didn't care. I was going to a dance with music and fun and it was going to be a wonderful time for all of us.

Little did I suspect that others in our community had different ideas and events that would happen at the gathering would alter my life forever.

* * *

There were sheep and wheat farmers there, so-called 'cockies'. The name came from their association with cockatoos and galahs hanging nearby their farms eating the seed. The feathered beggars had learnt to untie the sacks. The dance music and schedule of dances were overseen by the 'boss cockie', a bloke with a deafening voice which reverberated around the building.

As for the dances, there was a mixture of couples together enjoying Lancers Quadrilles, Circassian Circle, Irish Reel and the Scottish Reel as well. It was exhausting but jolly good fun. Those were interspersed with Polkas, Waltzes and my favourite the Varsovienne.

I recognised quite a few people there including the two troopers. Tweedle-dummer kept hedging for a dance yet I managed to always be saved by a more desirable bloke, usually Jesse.

Mr MacTavish spoke to me in an interval, asking if I'd heard any more regarding the theft of the gold samples that Archie had been sending to Wagga. Interesting. It was gold that the Major had stolen. How he'd discovered that the package was valuable was a conundrum to me. Why Mr MacTavish thought that I might be privy to information was another. Perhaps as it was exciting news, he was seeking gossip from whomsoever he met.

Seb also had his hands full to begin with but after four women limped off the floor complaining that his feet were squashing theirs, his dance card became very sparse. I eventually took pity on him and joined him in a polka Schnell. It was a big mistake and I retired injured within a minute. Seb was apologetic for his two left feet but those few moments in his arms I felt so comforted and safe. It was as though we belonged together. We took a seat by the front door in the quietest part of the hall. Most of the town was dancing or had chosen to head home as night was drawing in.

Whatever intuition prompted me to peek towards the door, I immediately tensed. Charlie Michaels had entered. He glanced around the hall then began striding in our direction. His eyes were fixed on me. I began chatting with Seb hoping that Charlie was able to observe that I was busy with another and had no interest in him.

No such luck.

'Come on, Missy. You're dancing with

me.' He grabbed my hand, pulling me to my feet.

'No, thanks,' I replied.

Although he was surprised at my reticence, his grip didn't lessen. By now others were aware of the fuss I was making. Seb pushed himself to his feet and Charlie sneered, ignoring the fact that they were of a similar build.

'The lady doesn't want to dance with you, mate,' Seb insisted. 'Be a good fellow and let her go or . . .'

'Or what, four eyes?' Charlie momentarily took his vice-like grip from my wrist and pushed Seb in the chest.

Unprepared as he was, Seb stumbled back, hitting a few empty chairs to fall, sprawling on the floor. He didn't try to get back up, drawing his legs into a foetal position in case Charlie laid into him.

Charlie grabbed my wrist once more and feigned a kick at Seb who cringed, covering his eyes. Not that I applauded fisticuffs and men slugging it out for the sake of showing who was stronger to claim a mate but I was disappointed at

Seb's lack of backbone to protect me. He couldn't face me from his prone position.

Expecting that my sole avenue of giving Charlie the message I wasn't interested was down to me, I steadied my feet. Jesse arrived and I felt proud that he did so. Shorter and lighter than Charlie he was standing up to Charlie. The thug released my arm and began to face off to Jesse.

The music had stopped and all eyes were on the two men. Where were the troopers? Then I saw them watching but doing nothing. Jesse was going to be in trouble as Charlie's reach was longer. I cried out for them to stop it at the instant a huge explosion with a flash of light and heat sent the two of them flying.

It was a moment later I saw a figure in dark blue dash by the open door towards a frightened horse. Outside flames of scarlet and orange enveloped the wooden terrace outside, liquid spreading across the wood with flickers of fire following. The pungent odour was kerosene. Black smoke billowed into the room as people backed away from the conflagration.

I heard Archie's voice yelling for water. The structure was wooden with an iron roof and would be alight in seconds, especially if that figure outside threw another bottle of kero.

Immediately, Jesse's commanding tones corrected him. 'No. Water will spread it. Bring buckets for sand or dirt. We'll smother it.'

There were woman and children, spilling out the back of the hall through doors and open windows as the menfolk fought the blaze with buckets and shovels full of dirt.

Charlie had vanished but Seb was on his feet sprinting for another door to the street that had been thrown open. The troopers followed him, presumably to try to catch the vile man who tried to burn us all alive. I realised now it was Major Midnight. He'd stopped in front of the windows for all to see, firing into the air to attract their attention. The attire and full head mask were unmistakable. Why on earth would he do this?

I reached the street behind Seb and the troopers. In the distance in the early twilight, we spotted the blue-clad bushranger galloping away. The troopers drew their guns but declared he was too far away. By the time they reached their steeds, he'd be gone, vanished it the night after which he was named.

Seb demanded a pistol from one of them, ignoring the claim that the arsonist was out of reach of any bullet. He passed me his glasses and aimed at the retreating rider, firing once. The rider continued for a split second before tumbling to the side of his horse.

The shot was 400 yards in fading light to a moving target. I'd never seen anything like it and neither had the gathered audience. There was quiet everywhere, the echoes of that single shot bringing all activity to a halt.

Then a woman, someone I hadn't met, gasped, 'Flaming 'ell. He killed Major Midnight!'

7

As Seb passed the gun back to the stunned trooper, he seemed to assume command. 'He's probably not dead. A few of you blokes go fetch him and bring the fellow back here. We need the doc too. This Midnight needs to answer our questions afore he hangs.'

He then staggered as if realising what he'd done. 'If you'll excuse me, I feel quite fatigued and dizzy. All that excitement and the fire.' He stumbled over a loose board as he began to make his way back to the oil lamp lit interior. The kerosene fire was out, with a few sand-covered, charred and smoking boards to show the near catastrophe for what it might have been.

'Damned fine shooting son,' an old-timer said, slapping him on the back. 'Let me buy you a drink. A proper one.' By tacit agreement, a keg of beer appeared and was placed on the bench by the lemonade and water that were the refreshments during the dance.

'Where are my glasses, Grace?' Seb asked. 'Blind as a flying fox without them.'

'Blind? But that . . . ?'

'Simply lucky. Reckon he fell off his nag at the fright of hearing the shot.'

I thought differently, having seen the calmness of a bloke in total control of what he was doing. It was, for a moment, an inconsistency. I passed him his spectacles, our gazes meeting momentarily in the flickering half-light of the lamps on the walls. His irises were a light blue, very light, almost grey.

He blinked and rubbed his eyes with his knuckle before he donned his glasses.

'You're . . .' I began before realising I couldn't be correct. Midnight was injured, possibly dead. He couldn't be standing in front of me as well.

The commotion outside grew louder until a group of local men, including the boss cockie, carried a very much alive bloke in dark blue in and laid him on a trestle table. Mothers shepherded their children away from the bloodied, groaning villain. I'd seen enough blood in the boxing ring, not to be perturbed by it. Seb's gunshot had struck him in the shoulder. The doc arrived with his Gladstone bag as Midnight's shirt was cut off to expose the injured arm.

'Are you going to use carbolic?' I asked him. He was surprised by my question.

'Why yes, young lady. Carbolic acid to stop any infection. I need to sterilise the wound and apply clean dressings after I clean my hands. It's much better than a slice of onion for stopping any germs. The bullet seems to have gone straight through. No bones broken. You have training in medical matters. A Nightingale perhaps?'

I'd heard of Florence Nightingale and her nurse training but I had to correct him. 'I'm aware of carbolic because I read of Joseph Lister's ideas. My father's a boxer. Dynamite Dan Stevens. I learnt about wounds from books and his doctor friends to help my dad recover better.'

At the same time, the arsonist's masks were removed. I didn't recognise him although others did. He was not the bloke who kissed me, not unless he was wearing a false beard.

Our doctor made an observation. 'Hello. What have we here? This man's been shot recently, a few days ago. A flesh wound that's quite infected. He'll have lost his arm if I wasn't around to treat it. Not that it will matter. Attempted mass murder. You'll hang for this Major Midnight.'

I decided to enlighten them. 'He's not Midnight. He's one of Charlie Michaels' men. Charlie shot him when he held up my stage the other day — a flesh wound right there. And look at the clothes. His hat's black, not blue. And there's no military insignia on his sleeve.'

A part of me breathed a sigh of relief.

Archie came forward. 'It don't make any sense for him to dress up as a rival bushranger — unless it was to discredit Midnight and his gang. There are folks out there shielding these outlaws for whatever reason. If they believed that Midnight tried to burn down this hall with all of us in it, they'd turn him in as sure as anything.'

Archie was right. I searched the assembled faces for Seb's, not seeing him anywhere. Upon asking Jesse, he replied that his companion had excused himself, revolted by the thought he'd injured a man. 'Seb abhors violence, Grace. He was outside, being ill. I'll go and check on him.'

Was that the real reason? Or was he avoiding me? As I waited, Mr MacTavish came over to me with a tall businessman at his side. Even before we spoke, I took a dislike to him. I wasn't in the mood for social niceties especially meeting the supercilious popinjay, yet the banker was insistent that we meet.

'Miss Grace Stevens. I take pleasure in introducing Mr Grenville Younger. He's a member of our Progress Association and a valued landholder and benefactor of the town.'

'Miss Stevens?' Removing his ostentatious top hat, he took my hand and raised it to his lips, bowing slightly. I pegged him as a swell straight away. 'A pleasure to see you here. I trust the evening's events weren't too distressing for a woman of your genteel disposition?'

'Quite the opposite. It was most revealing.'

One of the police came to interrupt him. The big fellow dismissed him with a harsh word.

'My son, Herman. Not the sharpest knife in the kitchen I'm afraid. Takes after his mother, may she rest in peace.' He noted my reaction. 'Oh yes, you would have met him and his equally incompetent brother after that stagecoach robbery the other day. We don't see eye to eye but I might give them one final chance to forget our past disagreements.'

The voice was strong yet measured, a monotone that conjured a vision of Satan speaking to Eve through the mouth of a serpent. His grey hair contrasted with black, bushy eyebrows that had a life of their own as they exaggerated every muscular twitch. Nevertheless, he was a powerful bloke, physically in addition to being one of the so-called landed gentries.

'Where in the States are you from, Mr Younger?' I asked.

'Georgia, Miss Stevens. The Peach State. I came over in the gold rush during the fifties and decided to stay to make this country my own, so to speak. But I must be off. It was a pleasure to meet you. I wish you and your school well.'

There were two men with him, the sort you'd prefer not to come across in a dark alley. He was gone before I realised, leaving us to ponder on the events of the night. From behind me, I heard a familiar voice talking to Archie at my side.

'Cui bono, Mr Applegate?' It was the Reverend.

'Beg pardon?'

The church official continued. 'My apologies. Latin for 'who benefits?'. It's what we should all be asking. Who would gain from having a bloke masquerading as Major Midnight fire-bombing this gathering? It would galvanise the locals to track Midnight down and kill him, no mistake.'

Since the answer was obvious to me, I said it aloud. I was sure others had reached the same conclusion. 'A rival bushranger? Charlie Michaels. By the way, where has he gotten to?' We searched the myriad of faces. He was gone.

It was the boss cockie who now voiced his thoughts. 'Damned coincidental if you ask me. Caused all that ruckus with you, Miss Stevens and your boyfriend. Close to that time, that fake Midnight threw the firebomb. As though he wanted us to be sure it weren't him.'

Seb came back in, to the cheers and claps of the assembled crowd. He thanked them in his usual unassuming way then asked me if we could all go home. By we, he meant Ma, me and Jesse.

Prior to us leaving, I had to speak to the impostor. His fate was sealed and he was fully aware of that. I ignored the grimace of pain. It was sheer good luck that no one was burnt or injured by his reckless actions. I had no sympathy for him. 'You, whoever you are. Who put you up to this? For goodness sake, man. There were children and babies . . .'

He stared back at me, his eyes becoming teary. 'Umble-cum-stumble, Miss.' It was not a phrase I'd heard often but it meant he completely understood. 'I . . . I just done what he told me, Miss. No one said I'd be shot . . . or hanged. I's following orders, that's all.'

I chose to press him. Of all the people close by him, I was the sole woman. 'Whose orders? Tell us. It may make a difference in whether you get jail or get hanged.'

His gaze darted from person to person, silently seeking help. No one offered. Then a confession, muttered with a sigh of resignation. 'Charlie . . . Charlie Michaels.'

★ ★ ★

I hardly spoke to Seb for the remainder of the evening or over breakfast. He,

142

wisely I might add, kept a low profile and avoided me too. It was an uncomfortable position that I found myself in.

We went to church together, though sat separately. The church was full for Reverend Peabody's inaugural service. Despite being prepared for a 'hellfire and damnation' sermon, the Reverend regaled us with uplifting anecdotes of his travels before Jerilderie. I enjoyed it yet wondered what the point was that he was making. It came when I least expected it.

He explained that joy can be found in the darkest and most depressing times in our lives but that evil might be there too, masquerading as our friends or benefactors, ready to destroy us at a moment's notice. Being nineteen, I was under no illusions that I understood people or the nuances of the games they played. In the view of the law, I was a child, not yet of age and certainly, unlike some women in our colonies, able to vote. In South Australia, propertied women were permitted to vote on local elections and there was a hope that the privilege might be extended.

At the rear of the church, there were a group of young women, shunned by the hypocritical men there as well as many women. Frau Schneider protected them as a mother-hen with her chicks.

I was tempted to talk with her yet chose not to. I didn't want my status or position as a teacher tainted by association at least not until I understood the politics of this small town better. It went against my gregarious, unjudgmental nature but it felt prudent. Perhaps a conversation with Matilda and Ma? I trusted their judgement.

Once we filed out of the church, I was brought back to reality. Seb bloody Longstreet!

He was an enigma yet I dared not confide my conviction to anyone that he was in fact Major Midnight. Should I turn him in and if so to whom? I trusted the Younger brothers as far as they could be thrown, despite their status as the local police. As for Jesse, dear sweet Jesse, he was The Captain — another deception that I'd been taken in by.

Last night had given me more questions than answers regarding the troopers. As the bogus Midnight was escaping, they made no move to stop him. He'd barely mounted his horse when we arrived, and they had stalled Seb until they thought 'Midnight' was out of reach of any bullet. They were wrong and the fanatical plan of Charlie to discredit the real Midnight had failed totally.

Charlie was now wanted; those protestations that proof was needed were no longer an issue.

I pulled Seb to one side as we exited the church. 'You and I need to talk, Mister.'

He nodded lamely. 'Somewhere private. By the creek. Two o'clock.'

I sensed an undercurrent of anger, not at me but at himself. He'd let that facade of bumbling quiet Seb Longstreet slip for a moment in front of me, letting me see his giveaway eyes. As Midnight he had disguised his head, hands, voice and pretended to be British. The one thing he couldn't cover were those tell-tale light grey eyes; hence the dark glasses and the light-sensitive vision excuse.

'Please tell me one thing. Were you and Jesse laughing at me being fooled?' I was angry too.

'No. You were the one person I wanted to tell. I . . . I care for you very deeply, Grace. I . . .'

I expected him to continue though he simply hung his head and ambled off alone towards Ma's. I stood there hesitantly, shaking my head.

'Lover's tiff?' Ma's question caught me unawares. She must have been watching.

'Far more serious than a tiff, Ma, and we're certainly not lovers. What would prompt you to suggest that?'

'Simply an expression, Grace. You could do a lot worse than Sebastian Longstreet.'

'That's the problem,' I mumbled, more to myself than her. 'From what I've discovered of our Mr Longstreet, I think he's the most deceptive bloke I've ever met.'

We rendezvoused as arranged, the bushranger and me. Our assignation was surreal as we sat by the glistening brook. Dragon and damselflies flitted and danced by. It was a lazy Sunday afternoon as we stared at the flowing waters, neither of us wishing to break the tranquil peace between us.

Finally, he lifted a flat stone and flicked it across the clear waters. It skimmed the water three times before sinking, sending circles of gentle ripples towards us.

'Why?' I asked, brushing a wayward lock under my bonnet. Those silver-grey eyes stared back at me as he rested the glasses on his thigh.

'We have our reasons, Grace. I'd prefer not to elaborate on them at this time. For your safety, you understand.'

It was a weak answer.

'For my safety? I should turn you in, you and Jesse. You killed a man. Or had you forgotten?'

He lay back on the grass, tipping his

hat to shade his rugged tanned features.

'See the clouds up there? The fluffy ones? I could watch them for hours, forget about the complications of life. They're not real you know, just wispy bits of nothingness drifting by. If you try to grab hold of clouds, you can't. While they tease you into believing they're tangible, they are as immaterial as a ghost. The troopers. They'll never find that man I murdered, whatever his name is. He's similar to those clouds, Grace. Ask yourself who told the troopers I shot him.'

What on earth was he saying? That he'd hidden the body, never to be found? Then it would be a case of Jesse's word alone.

I leant back on one elbow, confronting him as he brushed away annoying flies. 'Are you saying that you . . . that Jesse . . . he made it up? But that makes no sense at all. You're hunted for a murder that you never committed. That's senseless, Seb. Utter stupidity.'

He shrugged, returning my annoyance

with a sardonic smile, 'Part of a plot, a grand scheme. All I can ask of you is that you trust me. As Reverend Peabody said earlier, appearances can be deceiving.'

I pondered on that. The murderer who wasn't, the timid coward who failed to protect me from Charlie at the dance, the self-assured cavalier attitude of the bushranger who lifted his mask to kiss me passionately.

'That kiss? Was it real, Seb?'

'Shall we find out?' was his cheeky answer. He made no move towards me therefore the onus was on me to take the initiative.

I searched the surrounds to ascertain that we were alone. It was one thing to be embraced and be kissed, quite another to be the instigator. Did I wish to do this? Kiss a bushranger? It was not that he was forcing me and he did insist that appearances were not the whole story. I hesitated to make a decision. Under that disguise of a bumbling oaf who couldn't dance was a person I trusted and some-one to love. My pulse began to race as

I moved my arms to embrace him and hold my mouth close to his.

His cheeky gaze captured me as he whispered 'Trust me, Grace,' his breath tinged with parsley.

'I'm . . . I'm not all that good at this kissing thing,' I confessed.

'Neither am I. We'll have to learn together, Miss Teacher. Is that alright?'

I smiled and replied, 'Perfectly.'

* * *

A wonderful thing happened to me that afternoon. I lost my heart to the most gentle, affectionate and caring man I'd ever met. We kissed a few times. Actually, we kissed quite a lot but it was more than that. It was the closeness to him as we lay on the secluded patch of grass, his fingers stroking my wrist feather-lightly, his strong hand lifting mine to kiss my wrists and sensitive fingertips. We stared at the sky and the creek and the birds and wildflowers. Then we laughed or discussed our lives as children, experiencing the joys of nature in all its beauty. I loved his voice as he spoke softly.

We didn't discuss the here and now. By unspoken agreement, that was forbidden territory. Also, I did realise that being alone with a man, even in 1877, was far from the behaviour of 'nice' girls. Reputations were extremely frangible, subject to gossip and not-so-veiled innuendo.

Upon returning to Ma Huxley's we refrained from holding hands. Decorum ruled over passion and desire. Even at the dinner table, the undercurrent of affection was evident for both Ma and Jesse to see even if they pretended there was nothing out of the ordinary. There were no snide comments between Seb and I and that, in itself was notable. Once our fingers brushed each other's as we reached for the salt. I tried to keep my emotions in check but it set my fingertips tingling.

Seb was finished playing the fool and had left his trademark tinted glasses in his room. The need for pretence was over. Ma was acquainted with Seb from Bathurst and presumably was privy to his real nature. Whether she suspected him of being a bushranger, I doubted although his behaving in such an inept way must have appeared strange to her.

* * *

Having written in my diary, I lay in bed that night with two concerns on my mind: the first day of my new role as a teacher, and what had possessed me to believe that Seb and I had a future.

The school would take care of itself. First thing I would do would be to ask my pupils their names and then write them in big letters for us both to see. First names only. That way I wouldn't have to struggle with remembering who was who. Then we'd do a quick lesson on the alphabet, using the letters around the classroom with pictures and words to accompany each letter. A is for Apple. Repetition was the key to learning at least to commence with. Then we'd do what I did with that parent — David was it? By the end of the day, they would be able to write their name. True, they might need to copy it and would not recognise all the letters but it would come.

Seb, however? Well, he was another matter.

Technically he was a criminal. Technically. No one apart from me and Jesse realised that, consequently he was safe. He might have given himself away by shooting that bogus Midnight but I doubted it. Seb was a consummate actor. He had me fooled and I was closest to him these past few days.

But what future was there? If he gave up robbing stagecoaches and coach offices, he was a builder of bridges and, no matter which way one looked at that, there was a limit to the number of bridges that Jerilderie required. He'd move on while I was just beginning my life here.

Moreover, he was older than I. Maybe ten years, not a lot as far as marriages these days. My father was older when he wed my mother at seventeen.

I assumed that Seb was a learned guy, able to write and read as well as doing sums. Then why do a labourer's job on the Murray bridge? My head was hurting from thinking too much. I decided to use a little of the powder a friend of my father's had given me. There was a cup of water by my bedside. The combination of butterbur, ginger, feverfew and willow extract had worked remarkably well on the few occasions I'd required it.

My sleep was fitful, replete with dreams of Seb being arrested and put on trial. I woke in a state, my heart racing. What was I to do? By the time I prepared for school, it was approaching eight.

'Where are the boys?' I asked as cheerfully as I was able, considering my night.

'Gone. They had to leave early to collect the provisions from the store and blacksmith. Said they'd catch up with you soon and to wish you luck for today.'

I was upset. 'Nothing else?'

'Why no, Grace. Should there be?'

Had Seb decided that his life was

complex enough without adding a relationship to it? Or was this a normal pattern for men to follow?

I was wearing my apron to avoid dirtying one of the few frocks that I had and reached into the pocket for a hanky to dab my cheek. There was an envelope in there. Perplexed, I took it out.

'The telegram,' I exclaimed. 'I totally forgot it.'

'Who's it from Grace?' Ma asked pouring us both a cuppa from the teapot with the cracked lid. Then she tapped the strainer onto a plate then settled down to our shared breakie. Eggs from the chooks out back.

'Father. I wrote to thank him for the monies he hid in my clothing. A good thing too. That thieving scoundrel, Charlie Michaels, stole the rest of it in addition to my watch. I wonder if I'll ever get them back, maybe not the cash but the watch. It's precious to me. At least if Major Midnight had taken it . . .' I caught myself from adding that Seb would have returned it.

'What's the telegram say? On second thoughts, leave it for the mo. Your eggs will get cold.'

Ma was right. I tucked in. They were delicious along with the fresh bread made earlier. Finally, with one eye on the time, I touched my napkin to the edges of my lips and patted my tummy.

'I declare, Ma. I shall need to let my dresses out if I'm not careful with what I eat. I've never cooked myself. More an arsonist, burning everything I try to prepare. Papa did the majority of the cooking at home. I . . . I miss him.'

'But you can keep in touch. Letters and now telegrams. The miracles of this modern world. I've heard tell of a new-fangled gadget called a telephone where people can talk to each other over wires. Imagine that! Now, let's see what your daddy has to say . . . unless you want it to be private.'

I giggled. 'Of course not. I've known you less than a week, yet you're already like my second mother. I hope that doesn't offend you?'

She rose to come and hug me from behind. It felt right.

The telegram was short as you paid by each letter.

Beaut to hear you've settled in Grace Stop I'm well Hatter also Stop Did not put extra money in your clothes Stop Love Papa Stop

'That's lovely but who's Hatter?'

'My crazy snow-white cat. I called him Hatter after the Mad Hatter in *Alice in Wonderland*.' Then my furrow scrunched up. It was time to leave and now I had yet one more item to add to my long list of mysteries. I racked my brain, without success. If Dad didn't give me the banknote, then who did?

8

The day went well. In the end, I had four-teen children, some more eager to learn than others. Setting ground rules was the most difficult though I was opposed to using corporal punishment of any kind. In my opinion it did not work. There were other ways to control the unruly in class and, although scarcely five years older than two of them, growing up in Sydney had given to me a maturity and gifts that country folk lacked.

It was true that I couldn't milk a cow or skin a rabbit, freshly caught, for sup-per but I understood children and how to engage them. In between intensive les-sons on the three R's, I read to them, not British-based nursery rhymes as most of the pupils had outgrown such fantasies of faeries and wicked witches. I told them of bunyips and ghosts who haunted the rivers and billabongs of our land, stories I had written. They had heard of bunyips, of course, the Aussie version of boggarts and bogeymen, intent on capturing the unwary traveller or animal who chose to encroach on their territory as they chose to drink at a watering hole.

I then gave them pencils to draw what they imagined such a scene might be on the few pages of paper I had scrounged. They had writing on the back, wanted posters now redundant as the offending villain was banged up or dead. The Younger brothers had brought them over this morning as a gesture of goodwill.

Writing their names carefully at the foot of their completed drawing, each girl or boy placed their efforts on the wall, beaming at recognising their names and artistic achievements.

On another break, each of them told the class about themselves and their families. It was a social bonding exercise, although I could see from the furtive glances between the two eldest that they were in the throes of teenage love. I thought of Seb at that moment.

I might be able to educate my charges

on the subjects of a conventional school but who would teach me the mysteries of romance? I suspected it would be a difficult learning exercise, certainly for me. My emotions were stirred by hormones and sensations that could not be defined or written down for me to follow the guidance.

It was at lunchtime break that I sat outside, eating my sandwich with the younger ones that I watched my mature students running around. The exercise would be good for them, even though I suspected some of the boys were showing off for my benefit. As my lovely father once said, 'Boys will be boys, especially if a pretty girl be watching.'

I'd been paying little attention to the game, concentrating more on recalling names. Cuthbert was the one with the short blond hair and the slight limp, young Freddie was trying to keep involvement although he was barely six and Florence (who insisted on Flo) was screaming and pretending to be frightened. That intrigued me? Was this role model of terrified females something in our cells, a part of our constitution, or was it more likely learnt from those around us, our parents, relatives and friends? I believed the latter. I wasn't the hysterical timid woman I might at times pretend to be.

'What are they playing?' I asked one of the boys next to me.

'Bushrangers, Miss. Cuthbert is per-tending to be Major Midnight.'

'Pretending,' I corrected him, gently. Then I inquired why not Charlie Michaels?

'Golly, Miss. Don't you know nothing? Major Midnight is mysterious. He can be anyone who doesn't like rich people. Maybe he's my daddy or . . . or Reverend Peabody with a mask.'

It was food for thought. There were differences in who they stole from. In Midnight's case, it was the bank and Cobb and Co, although I was uncertain about Archie's package being stolen. Was Archie that rich? Maybe he would be, if he'd found gold as the banker suggested.

The end of the day came and as the children left my elation was spoilt a little when one of the littlies became upset because she couldn't read.

'My mummy said if I go to school, I'll be able to read,' she sobbed. 'But I can't.'

We'd had one day but sometimes expectations were unrealistic, especially in the thoughts of children. I had to explain it would take time like learning to cook and sew and that one day at school was not magic. She eventually smiled and spelt her name for me. It was a good thing it was Mary and not Elizabeth. Once she wrote it in shaky writing without copying, I put a little stamp on the back of her hand of a star. That brightened her cherubic face.

* * *

Alone that night with Ma Huxley, we had a simple salad with cold mutton and settled down to chat in the parlour with oil lamps to work by. Ma was doing some

162

embroidery of doilies but I had a puzzle to solve. It involved Seb.

I had my diary there, in which to write the facts. Just as I was ready to put pencil to paper, I had one of those enlightened moments. There was a niggly feeling regarding that bank note I found. I went to retrieve it and took the magnifying glass which Ma kept on the dresser.

'Pay the bearer ten pounds. Signed by the Gouvernor of New South Wales,' I read out to Ma who had placed her needlework on her lap. 'Trouble is, 'Governor' is spelt incorrectly,' was my observation.

'A forgery?' she mused, echoing my thoughts. I stood and took it to her with the curved glass. 'Yes it is, and a damn poor one at that. Where did you say you found it? Not your father as you thought?'

'No. It was loose in the clothing I brought from Sydney in one of the side pockets of a bag. Everything was strewn around when Charlie robbed us. A good thing he didn't take it. I just stuffed it all

163

back into the bag once he and his gang rode off.'

Her brows creased in concentration and she removed her glasses, on a chain around her neck.

'Ten pounds is an awful lot of money. Have you seen any other notes similar to that? Maybe they were mixed up with your luggage as you pushed your garments back into your valises?'

'Major Midnight stole a load of cash, The Captain stuffed it into his saddlebags. You don't think . . . ?'

I broke out into a broad smile. 'That Midnight stole a load of funny money? I wonder what naughty words he'll be saying when he realises the truth?'

Ma chuckled too. 'All that hard work for nothing. At least he can't be accused of armed robbery any longer. Fancy that! Charlie Michaels would be laughing his head off if he discovered the truth.'

'Yes, he would. Best not to tell him. Let him think that Midnight beat him to the cash.'

The jigsaw pieces were beginning to

join together even if I couldn't understand what the final image would look like yet. The cash that everyone believed Major Midnight had stolen was a lie. Also, the man with Jesse whom Midnight had shot was a phantom. Paul or Peter or Jeremiah didn't exist.

Logically, Jesse had made up the tale of his buckboard of goods for the bridge being hijacked. It was a charade, a flam. All to make the Major and Captain appear to be brutal outlaws, to be feared throughout the territory for their brazen and ruthless crimes. Mad Charlie Michaels had probably become Absolutely Furious Charlie, hearing of Midnight's ruthlessness. Charlie was no longer top dog. No wonder he'd tried to discredit Midnight last night in his attempt to turn the townsfolk against him.

'Heavens above!' I exclaimed. Seb (or Midnight) wasn't a hardened criminal after all. He was play-acting a dangerous part to rile Charlie. It was playing with fire. Charlie had a temper on him, no mistake.

Riling a snake was dangerous — it was far too easy to underestimate the snake's speed and bite.

However, a huge pressure lifted from my heart. The ambivalence I'd felt for Seb had gone. Right now, I wanted to hug him and kiss him until we both struggled for breath — but he wasn't here. Where was he . . . hunkered down for the night by the banks of the Murray with his fellow workers, or dressed in midnight blue plotting further mischief for Charlie? He and Jesse must have a secluded hide-out in the bush where they kept their jet-black brumbies only to change them for the sturdier horses which they used to haul the wagons.

Other jigsaw pieces clicked into place. That Wanted poster from Tasmania. I'd seen it. It had the same incorrect spelling — Gouvernment — undoubtedly the same printer as the counterfeit money. The cash was effectively children's play money that appeared real from a distance. It was never meant to fall into any hands but Jesse's and Seb's.

They'd put it on the stagecoach with the express aim for them to steal it and alienate the real bushranger who somehow was privy to that sensitive information. Charlie and his nefarious gang were not working alone and it was evident that those friends were in high places and living in Jerilderie, right under our noses.

I focused my gaze on Ma, who shifted uncomfortably, avoiding any eye contact. She stood, offering to prepare a warm drink before bedtime.

'Not so fast, Ma,' I said. She knew far more than she'd let on. Was she also a facet of this Midnight charade? After all, she'd let slip she and her late hubby had met Seb in Bathurst. 'You never told me what your husband did,' I said, asking her an unexpected question. 'And please, don't sell me a dog. I've had my fill of lies.'

She sat again, composed herself and faced me. The somewhat effusive mother hen persona made way for another woman whose eyes showed a hitherto determination and strength.

'Goodness. You are one clever woman, Grace. Bricky too, I've no doubt.'

I grinned. To be referred to as smart was one thing, brave and fearless quite another.

Ma continued, 'I'm glad you're on our side. My husband was a police officer, as was Seb. That's where we first met. Seb was starting out then but my Cyril and I saw straight away that he was a cut above the others. He was incorruptible. Clever too. Didn't do things by the book necessarily but by George, he got results. He was promoted to detective.'

My eyes opened wide. A detective? That explained a great deal. He was here to catch Michaels. No, that didn't make sense. A group of troopers would be able to do that. They'd done it before to other outlaws such as Captain Thunderbolt and Ben Hall.

'And what about Jesse? A copper, too?'

'No. He's an engineer, straight up. Works at Cobb and Co head office designing stagecoaches, bridges, whatever they need. It was the cover we needed for him and Seb to come. Jesse's very adept at turning his hand to anything, even stealing funny money with a mask and cover over that copper hair of his. It's taken weeks to put this charade together and little miss frilly-knickers unravels our secret almost straight away! If only Seb hadn't fallen in love with you at first sight!' She burst into a fit of laughter. 'Seb Longstreet. The toughest bloke I've ever met, turned into a love-sick bunny rabbit. I declare! Me and Jesse have had so much fun teasing him!'

I felt a tinge of pity for Seb, being tormented for admitting that he felt as much in love with me as I did with him. Moreover, learning of his secret life strengthened the affection I'd felt with that first touching of his lips on mine.

'Did you ask for him to come, Ma? Him and Jesse and that so-called gambler?'

'Oh, goodness. You sussed out that he's with us too? Yes, Arthur O'Shane. This is a big operation so we needed all the help we were able to get. There's corruption in this town, Grace, hiding in the most unlikely of places. Charlie Michaels and his gang are nothing. They steal the money but it's to fund something far grander than a night or two at Frau Schneider's, believe me.'

'Who else is privy to Seb and Jesse's true nature? I'm guessing Archie — am I right?'

I was on a roll and glad to be involved in this undercover scheme.

'Archie Applegate was despairing for months. He suspected there were rotten apples in this town if you'll pardon the apple metaphor. He approached me, aware of my history with the police. He's one of the few people I've shared my hubby's occupation with. Archie and me . . . well, it's not just you and Seb that spend private time together but I don't believe he thinks of me in that way, if you understand.'

She blushed the brightest pink I'd ever seen before composing herself and going on.

'Midnight has been around the Outback for a few months according to the rumours Seb started. He didn't want anybody to put one and one together with a new bushranger arriving simultaneously as Seb Longstreet did. A telegram now and then mentioning a masked robber in blue seen in Hay or a stranger in town mentioning Midnight's escapades set the scene for his arrival. It might seem a case of overkill to unearth what's happening in the area but it's important Grace — and it is working.

'Now that you're a part of this bizarre plan, Grace, you can help by listening and passing on information. I doubt that Jesse or Seb will be back until this weekend. Major Midnight though . . . well, we shall have to wait and discover what that dastardly villain has planned to confound Charlie and his associates.'

I had a restful sleep that night, knowing that Seb was on the side of the angels even though Reverend Peabody and everyone else thought otherwise. Nevertheless, as Ma Huxley had insisted, we

171

needed to be careful and keep a low profile. It was exciting yet terrifying at the same time. I felt the adrenalin coursing through my veins even now. At least I had found out the truth behind Midnight's actions. Or so I thought as I closed my eyes to drift into slumberland.

★ ★ ★

My second day at school was as rewarding as the first. Discipline was easier once the pupils understood my very simple rules. One thing I wanted to instil was respect, not solely for me as their teacher, but for one another, the older ones for the littlies and the boys for the girls. The reverse was true too. In an attempt to dissuade some of the boys from their hero-worship for bushrangers, I had a plan.

It was late morning when Frau Schneider arrived with a stranger in tow. As instructed the children stood and greeted them.

Frau took me to one side to explain.

'When I mentioned the school, Edward sounded enthusiastic and insisted on meeting you, Grace. I hope you don't mind. He has a meeting later today and has some time on his hands. He's from Victoria and is passionate about education.'

'Would you mind, Miss Stevens, if I were to watch you and your class?' He had an Irish accent as did many of the inhabitants of our area. We had all nationalities including Chinese, American and Italians. The gold rushes had brought many eager to find riches and better their lives.

'Feel free, sir. What do you do?'

'A log-cutter, Miss Stevens. I've moved around. It's difficult to find work if you can't reckon up or write. I saw that early in my life. My brother Dan and I are trying to better ourselves. The British make life hard for us Irish folk, even though I was born and raised in Victoria.' He grinned, barely visible through the thick brown beard that was down to his chest.

Frau Schneider took her leave as my

guest settled on a bench at the rear of the class. Having an audience bothered me not, as I had many overseers during my training years.

'Today, class, we're going to look at some letters. Tell me Katy, what is the letter with which your name begins?'

She answered and, once prompted, wrote her name on the blackboard. We gave her a little clap as she had done it without copying. Our guest joined in.

We then discussed the sounds 'C' and 'K' and looked at words beginning with 'K', like 'kite'.

'Sadly, English is very complicated,' I explained. 'A few words begin with 'k' that don't sound as though they do.'

I invited Edward to join in and show the knife I'd seen in a scabbard on his belt. 'Knife has a silent 'k'. I wrote 'knife' and 'knight' on the board and showed them drawings of both of them.

'Sometimes letters are silent. Just as you should be when I speak to you.' That caused a laugh, especially from the Victorian man.

'Why is the 'k' silent, Miss? Can't we leave it out when we write it?' Katy asked.

'It wasn't always silent, Katy. Words change the way they sound because people talk differently to how we used to talk.'

One boy said, 'Like my gran says 'thee' instead of 'you'. So does the Bible. And my prayers. 'Hallowed be Thy name, instead of 'Your name'.'

They were a bright lot.

I sounded the Old English way of saying 'knife' and 'knight', so they could understand that speech changes but spelling doesn't. 'Ke-neafay and ke-nick-tay.'

'Would you tell us all about these knights, Miss Stevens?' It was our guest. He'd come forward and was examining the drawings of the knights in their regalia with swords and shields. He held the picture book up for all the children to see.

'Of course.'

It was fine to have his enthusiasm. I planned to subtly change the play behaviour from bushrangers to knights and damsels in distress. Pretend swords in place of wooden guns.

I told them of King Arthur and the magical sword Excalibur, exciting their imaginations. All the time our guest paid avid attention, stroking that long beard of his pensively. Then he asked the craziest question. Wondering if he were joking, I exchanged glances with him but his narrowly set eyes remained serious.

'I doubt it. Those suits of armour worn by the knights of old were designed to deflect blows from swords, arrows and lances. I doubt they would have stopped a bullet. Maybe if the metal were thicker but that would make it very heavy to move around in. Why do you ask?'

'It's a thought, Miss Stevens, Just a thought. In any case, I must be going now. As for you kiddies, you must listen to your teacher and learn how to express yourself. After we have our new country, you will be the future leaders of our independent nation. Now I must be off to my rendezvous. I've come a long way to see this man and to enjoy Jerilderie's hospitality. You have a prosperous town, Miss Stevens . . . even a bank. I shall return here, one day soon.'

'Very well. Children, say goodbye to Edward.'

'Goodbye, everyone.'

I walked with him to the door. 'Sorry. My memory for names isn't very good, Edward. What was your surname, again, please?'

'I expect you'll learn it soon enough, Miss Stevens. My family and I are expanding our business into New South Wales to take advantage of the opportunities here. It's Kelly . . . Edward Kelly. But most people call me Ned.'

We shook hands and I watched him leave.

Ned Kelly? No, the name meant nothing. Still, there was a passion surrounding the man despite his strange ideas. A knight's armour, but bulletproof. Whatever next!

9

I told Ma Huxley of Ned Kelly's visit. Unlike me, she'd heard of him and his gang from south of the border. I felt quite stupid and explained that he was a charming fellow who had engaged with the kiddies very well.

'How was I to know he's wanted for robbery and murder?' I said. 'It seems that I must have a sign on my forehead inviting every bushranger in the continent to become my friend! What concerns me more is the reason that he's crossed the border to visit people in Jerilderie. What would be the business of a bushranger here?'

'A birthday party ... or a convention?' Ma's suggestions were less than helpful. 'Did he tell you who he was visiting?'

'No. I should have asked.' Some assistant policewoman I was! I was meant to help uncover the network of evil lurking in Jerilderie and not simply be a dumb blonde running about aimlessly.

'If it were secret, I doubt that he would have told you, Grace. Be grateful that you met Ned Kelly and lived to tell of it. He is not a fan of the establishment, especially the police force. There's a reward for his capture in Victoria and unlike Midnight's Wanted poster, his reward is real.'

* * *

During the following days, there were stories of bushranger activity from all directions around Jerilderie — another stagecoach heading south to Bendigo in the Victorian goldfields. It was attacked before crossing the Murray, still flowing swiftly with the runoff from the melting snows from the Kosciusko mountains.

'Was it Michaels or Midnight?' I asked Matilda as she spread the news one arvo after school.

'Michaels. There were three of them so it seems he has a recruit.'

The bogus Midnight who was the

third member of the gang was bound for Wagga Wagga jail.

Life in Jerilderie was busy, despite the size of the town. I didn't see Mr Kelly again and had no clue what he was doing in town.

Jesse arrived late on Friday in the buckboard but he was alone.

He was chatting with Ma Huxley in the parlour when I came home, keen to give my voice a rest after my first week of teaching. Most of my students had shown themselves to be human sponges, surprising me with their thirst for knowledge. It gladdened my heart, almost as much as the thought that Seb might be staying as well.

'No, Grace. He's not. Quite frankly, he and I are worried that our plans aren't working out. I'm aware that you managed to see through our subterfuge and that whatever conflict you felt for Seb being one of the bad guys has been put to bed, so to speak. But Charlie and his bosses haven't taken the bait as we'd surmised.'

Ma brought us a hot cuppa then joined us at the table.

'Bait? I don't understand?'

Jesse relaxed back on the chair then leant forward on the table, clasping his hands. His thick copper hair flopped over one eye.

'Archie. It was an outlandish idea to start with but we had to make them do something urgently, upset the well-thought-out scheme they've hatched. We thought if we could stir Charlie up first then throw a tempting morsel into the middle of their timetable, they'd make a mistake and we'd have them.'

My mind was already a jumble. 'Jesse. I have no idea what you're saying. Explain exactly what you mean because at the moment I'm going around in circles like as a one-legged duck.'

'A very attractive duck, I might add. And smart as a new button. If I weren't happily married to the sweetest Scottish lass, I'd be tempted to court you myself.'

I remembered him comparing his wife to a cockatoo and that she'd died.

Another lie to confound the criminals. A happily married bloke working on the bridge was more unusual than a carefree bachelor.

'Fair enough, Grace. Michaels is no one. He's a ten-a-penny bushranger who was recruited by . . . let's call them, The Conspirators. There are a lot of disaffected immigrants out there, people who came seeking a better life in the sun where they'd be tripping over nuggets of gold with every step they take. As you realise, that's not the case. The rumours of a fresh life with as much money as you want, spread throughout the United States and Europe, Asia too.

'So, they came, in their tens of thousands to a land that's one of the harshest and most hostile in the world. Drought, heat, poisonous snakes, strange creatures the size of a man that hop around. Then, to further complicate their life, the country is ruled by England. England! You can imagine how well they went down with some nationalities. Some colonies such as Victoria won't allow the Chinese in so they enter by South Australia and ride across the borders anyway.

'Each colony has its own rules and government and, quite seriously, it's bedlam. Imagine if some far-sighted people might expand on that chaos in an isolated part of the country that no one cares about, an area like . . . oh, like Jerilderie. Hundreds of miles from Adelaide, Sydney, Melbourne — in the middle of nowhere.

''Let's make a different country?' they decide. 'Call it Utopia, people it with immigrants, ex-cons, criminals of all kinds on the run from Victoria or New South Wales. You'll be safe. We'll make a country with a new government and we'll put ourselves in charge. And if there's gold or silver or copper under the ground, we'll claim it for ourselves.'

Jesse sat back for a breather.

'But . . . but that's sedition. England won't let them. They'll . . .' My thoughts trailed off.

Jesse fixed his gaze on me. 'Do bugger all, Grace. Pardon my language. They're twelve thousand miles away. What will they do? Send six ships with a thousand soldiers, arrive in Melbourne and march three hundred miles to fight a war? Hardly!'

I could understand his point and listened eagerly as he continued.

'Imagine that. Red coated soldiers marching along in one hundred degrees heat in a country most of them have never heard of nor even imagined in their worst nightmares.

'The soldiers they'll be facing have no uniforms or polite knowledge of how gentlemen wage wars. They'll be like the American revolutionaries. It would be a blood-bath, a rout. And England will not want that again.

'They rule countries like India and Australia, not by superior armies, they rule by pretending they're in charge so effectively that the other countries believe it. Once they lose a war in Australia, the myth of the British Empire will collapse like a pack of cards.

'The same with Sydney and Melbourne

and their soldiers. They'd capitulate since they would never agree on a plan to stop these conspirators. Hell, Grace, once Utopia declares its independence, they will have won without firing a single shot.'

I could not believe it. The hatred between New South Wales and Victoria was widely-known. They couldn't even choose the same gauge for their railways.

Ma Huxley spoke up. 'Our only chance is to destabilise this Utopia, or whatever it may be called, before it gets a stranglehold.

'The Eureka Stockade may have done the same thing back in 1854 — a different flag without the Union Jack, an independent country. It failed through lack of planning, although it did lead to political reform in Victoria including male and female suffrage.

'That rebellion failed to defeat the soldiers. This insurrection won't. We believe this organisation has been stockpiling weapons and ammunition for years. The trouble is we don't know who is the leader or where these armaments are.'

I'd heard of the Eureka Stockade, of course. Twenty-odd people killed, mainly miners objecting to paying 30 shillings a month for a mining licence in the Ballarat goldfields. There were over 120 detained and 13 brought to trial for high treason. They had been found not guilty and reforms were made.

The disaffected were Irish, Scottish, Norwegian and American. Peter Lalor, an Irishman who later became a member of parliament had been a leader.

It was a sobering few minutes for me. What I'd been told was unfathomable. This could not be happening to my home of New South Wales. All that I knew of my life and the lives of tens of thousands of my countrymen might be changed and I had no doubt it would be for the worse.

Jesse and Seb knew the identity of the bushrangers but the others were a mystery, as clandestine as the Illuminati that controlled much of European history from their shadowy refuges.

I decided to ask how Archie's stolen package fitted into all of this.

Jesse gave a smug grin. 'Ah, yes. Our masterstroke. Seb's idea originally but we all agreed we needed to stir things up, force them to act quickly and make rash mistakes. It was brave of Archie to volunteer to be the bait in our mouse-trap but he believes in Jerilderie and he's determined to stop this evil insurrection from happening.'

I had a few ideas regarding that. 'Let me guess. You and Seb rode into town, a brazen act designed to aggravate Charlie Michaels and his cohorts. Dressed as Major Midnight and The Captain, you made sure that everyone knew that you'd stolen valuable samples destined for the Assay office in Wagga. Consequently, Archie is privy to wherever the riches were found and it would be logical for anyone to force Archie to disclose where he'd found them. That's the cheese. He would lead the villains to the location and there you would spring your mousetrap.

After all, if you can't find where Charlie and his gang are hiding, why not bring them to you?'

Jesse's mouth opened in astonishment. 'I had no idea you were this smart, Grace.'

I blushed. 'I learnt a lot from my father concerning misdirection and getting your opponent to believe they're winning. Then they leave themselves wide open to a sneak attack.'

'Yes. That was the plan, but Archie hasn't been approached. Either Charlie hasn't realised there are rich pickings or they've decided not to chance kidnapping him. They have plans plus, we suspect, a huge collection of weapons and ammunition ready to arm their supporters. They've a timetable and it might be too much of a risk before the revolution.'

Jesse seemed worn out from the activities of the past few weeks. He smiled wanly.

'I hate waiting. If only we were able to find out who else is involved and the identity of the mastermind, we can swoop on them and arrest them before the fighting begins — not just Seb and me and O'Shane. Others wait for our signal.'

I tried to bolster his spirits. 'And now there's me too. I'm a part of your band of merry men. Maybe I can uncover some of these mysterious co-plotters for you. No one would suspect me.'

Jesse patted my hand and sighed. 'Yes, Grace. You can be our secret weapon. The trouble is, I doubt Seb would approve. He likes you a lot. And you're a bystander and this is not your fight.'

'He will want my help, Jesse. Just you wait and see. In the meantime, it's a waiting game. And I'm not a patient woman.'

★ ★ ★

Saturday morning saw me at the school rooms. There were no children to teach, however I did have one eager, though apprehensive, student.

'What if someone finds out what I'm

doing, Grace? I'll be the laughing stock of the town.'

'Why?' I said to Archie. 'Because you want to better yourself and learn? I reckon there are quite a few adults here in the same boat as you.'

Most people who had trouble reading and writing kept their secrets, pretending they were more literate than they were. Even in Sydney, in offices and on the trains, I'd spotted more than a few well-to-do gentlemen reading a newspaper upside down. They were oblivious to their error and I for one was reluctant to correct them. It was sad, in a way, that they needed to put on a show. At least Archie was brave enough to accept the help I'd offered. What he lacked in youth, he made up for in enthusiasm and, to be fair, he had the rudiments of reading there, awaiting my tutelage.

We had dispensed with nursery rhymes and banal stories concerning Jack and Jane. He was a businessman and wanted to be able to read order sheets and reckon up accounts. He was doing well too.

If anyone asked what we were doing, the story was discussing the school. His secret would be safe with me, even from Jesse, Seb and Ma Huxley. If I could help him on the quiet, I would.

I hadn't let on that I knew who Major Midnight and The Captain were or about his role in the grand subterfuge in which they were engaged.

There was a loud rap on the back door, the one backing onto Billabong Creek.

'Expecting anyone?' I inquired.

'Might be Zac, my foreman. Told him I'd be here,' Archie replied.

I went to answer it but as I reached for the handle, the door flew open, sending me staggering backwards. Three gun-toting masked men pushed past me, then headed for Archie. He was unarmed but stood up belligerently.

It was Charlie, I was sure of it. The masks were just for show and the criminal leader was wearing the same clothes as always. He was either a lover of grubby plaid red shirts and jeans or a man with a limited wardrobe.

'What do you want, Charlie? Run out of stagecoaches to rob because that Major Midnight beats you to it?'

Charlie swore. He was not in a good mood and hearing the Major's name didn't improve that disposition of his.

'No, Applegate. We came for you. We know you found gold and we want to have it for ourselves.'

'Yeah. What the boss said,' one of the minions echoed in a loud voice, trying to be threatening.

Charlie cast an irritated eye at his assistant bushranger but said nothing.

'What makes you think that, Charlie? Everyone realises there are no riches around here. Heaven knows, we've had our share of prospectors over the years. I'm telling you there's no gold, and even if there were, why should I hand it over to the likes of you?'

Archie might not be a strong man but, right now, he was one of the bravest blokes I'd met. The three gunmen had their guns pointed at him. I thought to make a break for it but, sensing my furtive glances at the open door, one of them grabbed me and pushed me down into a chair near Archie.

'Don't play games with me, old man.'

'Yeah, old man. Don't play games with us or ... or you'll be sorry.'

Charlie walked over and slapped his henchman on the back of his head, forcing him to lose his poorly fastened mask. He scrambled to retrieve it, almost giving me his gun to hold while he retied it. He gave his gun to Charlie instead.

'Sorry, Charlie. I can't tie knots real well and I'm all excited. This is my first kidnapping. Er ... I don't suppose you can tie my mask on again for me ... please?'

Charlie shook his head in exasperation. His apprentice bushranger wasn't doing too well. Charlie gave the gun back and the youth had no choice but to hold the mask over his face with one hand and his gun with the other.

If it weren't such a serious situation, I could have felt sorry for the recruit to Charlie's gang. It was obvious that bushranging was one of those professions that didn't attract a highly-trained group of men. Experienced bushrangers either had their gang or were in jail, awaiting the hangman's noose.

'Close your mouth, Bert, or this will be the first and last trip with my gang. As for you, Applegate, we know that package from the Cobb and Co office had gold in it.'

Charlie was angry but controlled. I had the feeling he was put up to this rather than acting on his own volition.

Bert couldn't help himself, still jumping around frenetically from foot to foot, waving his gun. He was so eager to please Charlie, I half-expected him to either explode with excitement or wet himself! 'Yeah. Applegate. You told the big boss about the gold you found. That's how we —'

'Shut up, Bert! For the last time, close that big stupid mouth of yours. You talk too much,' Charlie barked.

By now, Bert had gotten the message. 'Right, Mr Charlie, sir. I'll shut up . . . Won't say a word . . .

Won't even spea —'

Another whack to the back of the head.

Charlie sighed heavily. Being the boss of a gang of ruthless but also completely incompetent criminals was not an easy job!

'Now. Where was I? Oh yes. Applegate. We want that gold and you're going to lead us to it . . . or else.'

As one, everyone turned to Bert expecting him to repeat the 'Or else' but he didn't. He was too busy retying his bandanna, his gun shoved in the belt of his jeans. I hoped the safety was on, for his sake.

'What makes you think I'll show you, Michaels? I found it and the claim's registered in my name. You'll never get away with stealing it from me.'

'Oh, we will, old man. We got powerful friends. And after R-Day, all your claims will be worthless anyway. The gold will be part of New Eden.'

Then, as if realising that he'd said too much, Charlie took a step towards

Archie. 'You're coming with us, otherwise I shoot Miss Teacher, right in front of you. Understand?'

Archie didn't hesitate to comply, begging Charlie not to hurt anyone. He said he'd show them the location of the vein of gold he'd found but it would take roughly eighty minutes to get there. They were ready to file out to the horses outside, but Bert was upset.

'Oh, gees Charlie. I expected more shooting and stuff. Can't I shoot the teacher anyway? Pretty please?'

I shuddered. Bad enough that Charlie was barking mad but it was evidently contagious. All of a sudden Bert wasn't funny any longer.

'Absolutely not. I quite fancy her myself but another time. The gold's the priority now. Reckon she'll fancy me more than that four-eyed wimp she was with at the dance.'

Bert pouted but left, warning me not to raise the alarm until they were well on their way. Not that I expected the police to do anything. I had to find Jesse and tell him what had happened as quickly as possible.

Rushing out the front door I spotted the bushrangers and Archie on a fourth horse they'd brought for him. They were exiting Jerilderie through almost deserted back streets.

Where could Jesse be? Hurrying back towards Ma's I heard his voice from inside the blacksmiths. He was probably overseeing more metal fittings for the bridge. He noticed me straight away, perspiring and breathing heavily.

'Grace. What's happened?'

I went back outside, keeping in the shade. Jesse followed me.

'Archie . . .' I began to weep. 'The– they've taken him.'

Jesse's face lit up. 'Why that's wonderfu —' he began then noted my look of terror. He came to me, burying my face in his shoulder as he started to comfort me. 'Sorry, Grace. I wasn't thinking. It would have been dreadful for you to see.'

'He was with me when Charlie arrived. He's in terrible danger.'

As he stroked my hair, Jesse wiped the tears from my cheeks. 'Grace. Listen to me. They need him alive and unhurt. All they want is the location of the precious metal he said he found. Did they say what metal?'

I was perplexed. 'Gold. They said gold.' Why was he asking this?

Jesse nodded. 'Right. That makes sense. We always thought he was involved. Now, did Archie say how long it would take to get there to where the gold is?'

Another strange question. 'Eighty minutes and they left five minutes ago. Come on, we can catch them and save Archie.'

'Eighty minutes. He's taking a long way and he'll be slowing them down. It'll take me half that time through the pass. I'd better warn Seb that they're on their way.'

'You mean 'we'? I'm coming with you! We can borrow two horses from the Livery Stables and —'

'Whoa there, Nellie. I can't let you do that. And I'm bloody sure I'm not having a woman slow me down. This is dangerous business and I'm not nurse-maiding you in that dress riding side-saddle like it's a jaunty picnic in the country.'

I wiped the last tears from my face and fixed my gaze on him angrily, my teeth momentarily clenched. He was being protective but he was also being patronising. Men!

'I can outride you any day, Jesse. I've won best horsewoman at the Sydney Royal Easter Show the past two years and I can rope as well as any man. Just get me a half-decent horse around 15 hands-high, preferably that dappled grey brumby I saw the other day. A man's saddle. I'll go and change. Five minutes outside Ma's.'

He stared at me, breaking into a grin. 'Five minutes then, Grace. Hope I don't regret this.'

'You won't, Jesse. Just try and keep up when we start. I hope that Seb isn't too surprised to see me there.'

If I'd realised what his reaction would be, I would have stayed in Jerilderie. I thought I understood the man. What happened later showed me how stupid and naive I was.

10

Galloping across the open countryside to the west of Jerilderie, I had to rein in my stallion and my eagerness to let Jesse lead the way. We both had brumbies, Australian wild horses from up in the Snowy Mountains. These feral horses were great for endurance riding, sure-footed and smart as any horse I'd ridden. They were our equivalent of American mustangs.

Where we were heading was a rugged countryside away from the wheat fields and sheep grazing land around Jerilderie. Jesse told me it was out west of our town. He was familiar with the way overland which is why we would beat Charlie's gang there.

As we paused for a drink from the canteens he'd thoughtfully brought along, he surprised me by saying, 'You're amazing, Grace.'

'Thank you but you're a married man.

Let's keep our relationship professional, Jesse.'

He spluttered and almost choked as he began laughing.

'No. I meant you're Amazing Grace. Watching you mounting Grey Ghost here, I realised that I saw you performing at the Royal Agricultural Show this year. My wife, Betty, was there too. They had your photo in the Morning Herald. 'Amazing Grace' they called you. Wait until I tell Seb and Betty.'

'I'd prefer you not to mention that particular name to Seb. It's part of the reason I came out here. And if you dare start singing that song —'

'Yeah? You'll what?' he dared me.

'I'll think of something extremely nasty and painful. Trust me. It's bad enough that guests at dinner tables point at me and chant 'Grace' in unison after some halfwit suggests saying grace before the meal. I would prefer to think that, as a friend, you might be more circumspect. After all, Jesse isn't exactly a name without criminal connotations, is it?'

'Point taken, Miss Stevens. From now on I'll call you Mediocre Grace.'

'Much better. How far to go?'

'Our destination is in those hills just to the right. A blind canyon in the middle of Wombat Ridge. A perfect trap for our bushranger friends. Charlie and his gang are riding straight into it. Shall we . . . ?'

'Hyah,' I said to Grey Ghost, urging him on.

Jesse didn't waste time either. We'd be in place with Seb well before Archie led them into the blind canyon from the other side.

Jesse told me there was an abandoned mine there but no gold. The aim was to entice Charlie's gang then capture them, hopefully without bloodshed. Following that, the authorities and their team could move in on the others in charge of the planned insurrection.

In a way, it was as exciting as the day before one of Papa's big fights. There was always a chance he'd be hurt but one thing he'd taught me over the years as I sat watching him spar, was that preparation was the key to success.

Papa had had spies studying his opponents, watching their techniques as well as their training schedules. Whether a few of them suspected that they were being observed by the opposition didn't matter. Dad had his sources. He'd find out what they had for breakfast, if they had an injury or weakness that he could exploit, even if they or their girlfriends and wives were being unfaithful.

'I'm eight years older than the bloke who wants to take my Heavyweight belt from me, Grace. I need to understand my opponent better than his dear old mum. If I can't predict exactly what he'll do in that first round, I've lost the bout.' Then he'd guffawed in that deep belly laugh of his. 'You remember that fight last month?'

'The one with Knockout Nolan? He had you on the ropes in the second round. Then he seemed to lose any self-control. He was lashing out all over the place then you put him down with that left-right combination. He's still seeing stars.'

'Want to find out what happened?'

I nodded.

'I whispered that I'd seen where his wife's birthmark was when we'd made love the week before. Sneaky and underhand but there's nothing in the Queensbury Rules about that.'

Dad gave me a cheeky wink as I laughed.

'And had you seen it?'

'Sorry, Grace. There are things a father doesn't admit to his favourite daughter. But Nolan believed it and I beat him. Sometimes you have to win, by whichever way you can.'

Bringing my mind back into the present moment, by this time, the terrain was rugged and hilly and covered by treacherous bandicoot holes.

Jesse's mare almost bolted as a snake reared its ugly head, hissing away. Galloping was out of the question. It might have been quicker to walk with the horses in tow but I was confident in the two brumbies.

'Our supply cave is half a mile further

on but this is where we planned to over-see the capture of Charlie's gang. Seb and two of our men were waiting here all week for Charlie to take the bait.'

As we approached what seemed to be the destination, Jesse made a currawong sound, a bird call that presumably announced his arrival. Actually, our arrival. I was confident that Seb would be as happy to see me as I was to see him again.

A bloke I didn't recognise appeared from behind a wizened scribbly bark gum and gave a thumbs-up sign. Then he pointed to the right.

'You go with Johnnie while I hide the horses. Don't want their whinnying giving the game away when Archie leads them here.'

I dismounted nimbly, passing my reins to Jesse. It was a hard scramble up the steep slope. Johnnie, a man of few words, ushered me further up the rocks to the top where I could see the blind canyon below.

'Get down, Jesse,' Seb whispered.

'Wait . . . you're not Jesse. Who . . . ?' He was in his dark blue garments, save for mask and hat.

I ducked and removed my own hat, shaking my long hair free of its confinement.

'Grace! What the hell? You shouldn't be here.'

'Archie's been kidnapped. They're on their way,' I replied, ignoring the angry, irritated tone in his demeanour. 'Three baddies including Charlie. I . . . I thought you'd be pleased to see me, Seb?'

A welcome kiss was out of the question with Johnnie there but, even then, a peck on the cheek or the hand, surely?

The look that Seb was giving me reminded me of Papa's furrowed brow when I'd decked that bully at school. Explaining that the nasty little rat warranted it for picking on my friend didn't change that disapproval.

'But he deserved it, Papa!'

'I've no doubt he did, Gracie. But you shouldn't have done it in front of the school, teachers too. You humiliated him in public and he'll hate you forever. Moreover, your classmates will treat you differently — good and bad. They'll be afraid of you and the teachers will call you a trouble-maker.'

'Are you saying I should have ignored what he did to Miriam? Let him off scot-free?'

His angry gaze had softened. 'No. Of course not, sweetheart. Just that you should have done it differently. Remember, you're a girl. A very special girl, right enough, and you can use that to your advantage but remember to —'

'Choose my battles,' I acknowledged, repeating his maxim. 'What would you have done?'

He had mused on that for a moment.

'Firstly I would have tried to convince him of the error by talking. Fighting is a last resort. Then, if he refused to change his ways and apologise publicly to Miriam, I would have fought him, but somewhere private. Just the two of you. That way you'd avoid humiliating him in front of his mates, and not get yourself a reputation in the school.'

'But Papa. He'd tell everyone I beat him up.'

Papa had ruffled my hair then. I'd brushed it till it was golden shiny and had spent ages arranging it but I didn't mind. I had loved my big woolly-bear dad so much.

'Use that brain of yours and plan things, Gracie. Would this boy do that?' he had said.

I stared at my hands. The bruised knuckles from the fight were fading quickly. Then I grinned. 'No, Papa. Being beaten up by a girl? No way would he admit that. It would be our secret.'

How would Papa advise me to deal with Seb, I wondered? Now, I turned to look at Seb.

'Sorry, Seb. I wanted to help you capture Charlie's gang, that's all.'

It was time to be Miss Meek and Timid, I sensed. At least for the moment. Me turning up like this must have been a shock as Seb was focused on executing the scheme to capture the bushrangers as safely as possible.

'Good grief, Grace! What were you thinking? And what's all this — dressed like a bloke, jeans and all?'

His eyes roamed over my body, resting on my exposed neck. Realising that, I hastily fastened the top button. He coughed and stood, turning away, relieved when Jesse clambered up from the slope away from the steephead ravine.

Seb didn't wait before commencing to berate him for bringing me.

Jesse tried to reply but was shushed as a fourth person climbed to our collective vantage point.

'They're coming, Seb. Keep your voices down. These canyon walls carry echoes everywhere.'

Seb nodded, indicating that I should crouch out of sight and keep quiet. He completed his ensemble by donning his face covering, mask and hat. I guessed Jesse had his disguise on too.

Great! I wasn't even allowed to peek as they'd ride up the flat-bottomed valley to the end. Presumably, the make-believe gold mine was there, though I had no idea how Seb's team planned to capture them. A gunfight would endanger Archie who would be guiding them.

I sat there huddled behind a boulder, looking out the way Jesse and I had come from. We were high up, the horizon sky bluing into the barren plains below.

Sometimes, I hated being a woman! I was strong, able to box and ride and rope better than most men I'd met, yet in the eyes of society, I was a second-class citizen. Showing what I could truly do made men afraid and resentful. It was my father who'd kept bolstering my ego and telling me not to take notice of the perceptions of others.

I'd prayed that Seb was different yet it appeared that I was mistaken.

I was to be cosseted and protected simply because I was female. My fighting and scheming skills would be dismissed as insignificant as a gnat was to a horse.

There was silence from the other side of the boulders as Seb's team watched the approach of Charlie's men, wending their way through the valley below. Charlie's gang should be wary yet they weren't. I heard their bravado and arrogance from here, boasting that Archie's treasure trove of gold ore would soon be theirs for the taking. Once found, would they kill him?

I believed so. But until they were certain that he'd led them to his hoard, he'd be safe.

★　★　★

'Perceptions, sweet Gracie. Life is all about perceptions. You can use that to your advantage. People see you as lithe and pretty, a weakling woman. You're not. It's like with me, Dynamite Dan, 'the man with the explosive punch'. Can you imagine all those billboards if I changed my name to 'Pussycat Dan'?'

I'd laughed. Papa's fondness for cats didn't fit his image even though it was evident when he played with Hatter.

'Pretending to be the 'little woman'

might satisfy most people you meet but one day there will be a bloke who will come into your life. He will be the one who you can share your real self with and he'll love you all the more for it. Be patient. Finding him will make your life complete.'

I'd thought that bloke might be Seb. How stupid could I be? He hated me, even felt disgusted to find me in men's clothes. And now, I was shoved aside while the four men took charge of Operation Goldmine.

The raised voices mingled with the clip-clopping of horseshoes on the rocks below.

'How much further, old man? My backside's getting sore from all this riding.'

Archie answered, 'Just around the next bend. The disused mine's there in the limestone.'

He sounded tired and scared. Whether it was an act for their benefit or the fear that Seb and the others might not be there, I wasn't sure. All I did was cross my fingers and pray that the operation panned out.

They all dismounted and proceeded on foot. I was surprised not to hear Bert's voice repeating everything that Charlie was saying like a demented parrot. Perhaps he'd learnt his lesson to be quiet although that was unlikely. Bert struck me as the hard-to-train sort.

'It's in the mine shaft going into the hill at the end. A hundred yards on the right. You'll need to watch them timber supports. I haven't finished shoring them up yet, not expecting visitors and all,' Archie drawled.

Good ol' Archie. His sarcasm was lost on the three stooges but at least he wasn't beaten down by the situation.

'I'll go on first,' he offered.

'No you won't, old man. You'll probably collapse the tunnel hoping to take us with you. George — you stay with him out here. We can finish him off once we check he's not lying. You got the lanterns?'

I heard a mumbled 'Yeah' then lots

214

of metal being bumped around as they picked up the lanterns and two moved off.

The voices were more distant.

'Go on, Davo. Don't tell me you're afraid of the dark?' said Charlie.

Hold on, I thought. Something doesn't add up. I dared not move or even whisper a warning but Seb needed to be told.

The silence seemed to drag on forever then George, the bloke with Archie, swore. Some words about what was taking so long and Archie had better not be joshing them on a wild goose chase. He'd hardly finished when there was a cataclysmic bang from underground!

As I had to see what was happening, I inched around to the secluded hiding space overlooking the canyon.

Down below through a chink between boulders, smoke was billowing from the mine. George was cussing again, demanding for Archie to show himself. I changed my vantage point as Seb along with the others made ready to fire at George.

Archie had vanished, leaving George alone. He was frantically searching the boulders and crevices for Archie while trying to watch the mine entrance.

Archie must have slipped away into some preordained hiding place away from his captor, the second that the explosion sounded. It was planned!

One of the men with Seb fired a shot at George's feet. 'Throw down your gun. You're outnumbered and a sitting duck, mate.'

George reacted as expected. He fired wildly up to the cliffs on both sides, missing us by a country mile. The echoes made it impossible for him to pinpoint the source of the shouted command.

One more bang and another puff of dirt at his feet, closer this time. He was wide-open to Seb's men. He jumped.

'Last chance, Sunshine! Lose that colt or next time we won't be aiming to make you dance.' It was Seb this time, having raised his kerchief to be heard more distinctly.

Once more, George scanned the rock

faces in the vain expectation of spotting his assailants.

Like a skittish rabbit, he fired again at shadows before accepting his fate.

'Hold on, hold on. I give up! Look . . . tossing my gun away.' The weapon clanged against a rock, landing five yards distant on the sandy dirt floor of the valley.

'And the other one, Georgie Porgie. Be a good man, now. I'm Major Midnight, after all, and I'd kill you as soon as blink.'

Seb had stood, ensuring that George would notice him glaring from the rugged cliffs, forty feet above him. His mask and hood struck terror into Georgie more than the voice had, but to his credit, the outlaw tried to ingratiate himself with Seb, almost changing horse in mid-stream.

'Oh. It's you, Major. Thank the Lord for that. I thought you might be troopers. But you're one of us. In fact, I was just thinking about joining up with you and dumping Charlie. Moving up in the world so to speak.'

He grinned, his missing and crumbling teeth visible for us all to experience.

Checking that George was no longer a threat, Seb hollered, 'You can come out, Mr Applegate. We have no argument with you, only these thieves trying to steal our gold-mine.' Seb emphasised the 'our', openly implying that he and Archie were partners.

Archie appeared from his hiding place. 'Sorry, Mr Midnight, sir. They forced me to come; threatened the school teacher lady too.' Archie gathered the guns and carried them over to Jesse, himself masked and garbed in blue. Jesse had descended to confront George.

Seb wasn't finished.

'As for vacancies in my gang of bushrangers, George, we don't have any. I already have over a dozen men, most of whom are busy elsewhere.'

At that point Seb's two accomplices stood, their faces also covered.

A dozen? What was he up to? Was Seb a pathological liar, incapable of telling the truth? I doubted that. But why the continued charade? I was certain that the two blokes standing mere feet from me were all there were. Why pretend otherwise, especially since George was effectively under arrest?

Whatever was going on, I didn't want to upset the elaborate strategy but I still had to tell somebody that there was a problem. I beckoned one of Seb's men to kneel by my side permitting me to whisper my warning. He nodded to me but was distracted by the sight of activity at the mine's entrance.

'They're coming out Major. Reckon their heads will be ringing for a month. That army booby-trap we set in the tunnel did the job all right. 'Flash! Bang! Wallop!' It certainly lives up to its name.'

I wondered if the 'flash' part referred to exploding magnesium powder, the stuff that they used in flash photographs. It explained their apparent temporary blindness.

He and his companion scrambled over the boulders like cats, alighting on the flat floor and dashing to the mine, guns raised and pointed. By this time, Charlie and his accomplice had managed to crawl on all fours from the hole in the hillside. Even from where I was, it was evident that any fight had been taken from them.

Seb's helpers took their guns as they writhed and moaned, hands covering their ears. They'd not been blown up then; just a sort of loud bang, amplified by the narrow confines of the tunnel.

Their hands were quickly bound and they were frogmarched back towards Jesse, Archie and the third captive.

However, he'd managed it, Seb had captured Charlie's gang without any injuries. And that devious design of his wasn't complete yet. I should have stood to warn him of the one possible hassle but a sixth sense warned me that my high-pitched female voice might ruin his grand design.

'Pssst!' I whispered.

At first, Seb ignored me. Possibly his hood muffled sounds. I had to persist.

He thought that it was all under control but I was worried. I tried again, tossing a stone at his boot. That got his attention.

Against his wishes, he bent his head to listen to my hushed words.

'There's a fourth man called Bert. He was there when Archie was taken. But he's not here now. I don't see him.'

'Are you certain?' Seb was concerned. He moved away from me to call the others. 'Guys. We might have a slight problem . . .'

I stretched, cramp setting in from the long confinement. Suddenly I was yanked to my feet from behind, rocks all around apart from the few square yards of flat ground where we'd secreted ourselves. Someone's hand was around me, hugging me tightly in a most inappropriate fashion. I tried to struggle but my assailant told me not to move, his fetid breath grazing the side of my face. His other hand pointed a gun at Seb who began to reach for his weapon.

'Not so fast, Midnight — if that's who you are.'

It was Bert's voice, hesitant and scared but confident that he had the perfect shield holding me. I felt his grubby fingers on my body and hated him all the more for it.

How cowardly, to be hiding behind a woman's skirts — or pants, in this case — but he was outnumbered. Mentally I kicked myself. I'd warned Seb and Jesse there were three kidnappers. I was mistaken. The fourth one must have joined them as they rode out of town with Archie. Bert had lagged as they'd approached the mine, probably as a back-up in case things went belly-up. They had done, meaning Bert felt it was now his job to save them.

'What do you want, son?' Seb asked, calmly lowering his weapon.

'I'm not your son. I'm a growed up man, and I . . . I want you to let my friends go . . . either that or I shoot you and throw this woman over these rocks.' He'd backed me up to an open part overlooking the plains from where Jesse and I had approached.

It was a long, very bumpy way down. I gasped.

From the blind valley, Jesse called up. No one down there could see us or the predicament we were in. 'Major. What's happening up there? Should we come up?'

'No. Stay put. We have a situation. Another member of the gang. He's . . . he has a hostage. And demands.'

Bert was edgy, moving his feet from side to side, that gun in his hand wavering all over the place. It was a bad combination, fear and a gun but worst of all was him behind me, his head brushing against my hair as he peered out either side at Seb.

'Last chance, Midnight. Tell your friends to let my gang go . . . or else.'

A stalemate, neither man willing to concede defeat. It was up to me, Miss piggy-in-the-middle.

Hoping to catch Seb's eye, I gave a discrete nod which he returned. My mouth was dry and I felt violated by the creature holding so tightly.

Here goes, I told myself silently.
Then all hell broke loose as he fired.

11

My throat was dry and my heart was pounding like a bass drum but I was focused on what I must do.

As I sensed Bert's head move behind mine to glance from the other side, I smashed my boot heel hard down on his toes. Simultaneously, I pushed his lower right hand into the air with my left. The gunshot almost deafened me, my ears ringing from the noise, yet I gritted my teeth and brought my right elbow backwards with as much force as I was able to muster. Something cracked. I hoped it was his rib and not a part of me.

Next thing I felt was him release the gun and my chest-hold as he doubled-up in pain.

Almost in slowed motion, I noted Seb sprinting forward as I spun around to confront Bert. His mouth was open in shock — or pain. I didn't care which. He'd touched me where I objected to being touched and a broken rib or two was just the start.

My right hand closed instinctively as I let fly with a right hook. Bert's head snapped to my left as it was struck then the would-be bushranger tumbled against a boulder, a tooth flying out from his mouth.

I paused for breath, bending forward to put my hands on my knees. There was no need to check. He'd be out cold. Damn — I'd lost my temper. I should not have done that despite the provocation.

Seb quickly knelt to check the carotid pulse in Bert's neck.

'Is he . . . ?'

'No, he'll live. Great Scott, Grace! That was amazing,' he said and without thinking, pulled his hat, hood and mask off.

'Yeah. That's me. Amazing bloody Grace,' I answered in a quiet monotone.

Inwardly, I was shaking. The anger — that wasn't me. Or maybe it was. He might have been killed — by me.

It didn't matter that he'd threatened my life and Seb's. It was my actions . . . the rage. At that moment I hated myself more than I ever had.

And Seb had seen that, the anger, my clenched teeth, the desire to hurt. No wonder he made no move to comfort me. Not that I wanted that in any case. He'd already made his contempt for me as an equal evident.

Only now could I hear the shouts from below and galloping hoofbeats fading into the distance.

Jesse appeared from climbing up. 'Everyone alright? We heard a gunshot . . .' Then he noticed Bert spread-eagled on the ground. A trickle of blood ran across his cheek.

Seb stood immobile, staring blankly at Bert. He was almost mesmerised, unaware of his surroundings.

Jesse shook him by the shoulders. 'Seb. One of them got away in the confusion, just as we figured.'

After a second or two, Seb moved.

'What? Got away? That's good. We'll

take this one and the others to Wagga. Telegraph the troopers there to meet us on route then we can return and sort this insurrection out once and for all. Tell the rest to be ready to move early next week.'

His voice was subdued and cold. There was no emotion, simply a grim determination.

'What about Grace? She's worked it all out, you realise — who we really are, what we plan to do. She's one clever woman, Seb.'

'And she almost got herself killed. Just like . . .' Then he stopped his musings and stood up straight, composing himself as the man in charge.

'Send her and Archie back to town. We have Charlie and his gang in custody. The beginning of the end — hopefully.'

'And the one who made his escape?' I asked, nursing my bruised knuckles.

'It doesn't concern you, Grace. None of this does. You'd best leave us to tidy up.'

What? Not even a polite thank you for flattening Bert and possibly saving his life? I was seething underneath but I was damned if I'd allow him the satisfaction of seeing my hurt. As he said, it was better if I returned to Jerilderie with Archie. It'd be a snow-filled day in January before I concerned my life with Seb Longstreet again. I was grateful our liaison was brief. It had been a valuable lesson.

* * *

We made our way to the canyon floor where Charlie and his fellow bushranger were slowly recovering their sight and hearing. I was lucky there was a narrow winding path to descend as scrambling down the forty-odd feet of rugged boulders would have been more precarious than climbing up. Unlike the men, I was not part mountain goat. Jesse had gone to retrieve our two brumbies and Bert's horse for the circuitous route into the valley where we were all meeting.

Seb had Bert slung over his shoulder like a rag doll. He and I didn't speak.

Eventually, we were all together: Archie, Seb and his three teammates along with Charlie's gang. Archie was shaken though not as bad as Charlie. That 'flash, bang, wallop' booby-trap had done its job.

Charlie stared at Seb in his Major Midnight garb and the rest with their hoods on. His hands and feet were bound securely.

'You're Midnight, eh? What you going to do with us? Get rid of the opposition? Steal all the money for yourself? Be warned, Major. We's got mighty powerful friends in Jerilderie. Pretty soon this will all be part of another country, New Eden, and you'll be the ones hunted down and killed.'

'These friends of yours, Charlie. Who are they? Maybe I can make a deal with them like I did Applegate here?'

The Major was standing with Charlie helpless at his feet. Despite my feelings concerning Seb, in his disguise, he was an imposing figure, confident and playing the part of a fellow bushranger to perfection.

'I'm not telling you. And what did you do with Bert? He was our back-up plan in case Applegate tried to get away.'

'Oh, Bert? The school teacher knocked him out. She's got quite a punch.' It was a compliment that made me feel better about my actions.

Charlie squinted, the midday sun making it difficult for him to focus. 'Bloody oath. It's the teacher all done up as a bloke. Didn't recognise her. What's she doing here, anyways? She your girl-friend?'

Neither Seb nor I responded to that although we did exchange a fleeting look.

'Suppose I tell you what I know about you and your powerful friends, Michaels. Then I'll let you in on a secret and what me and the men have planned for you.'

Charlie forced himself to sit, leaning on one elbow. He stared at Seb and the three imposing blue masked men. Although Jesse, or The Captain, was more slightly built, Seb and the other two were tall, muscular and professional.

Charlie must have been ashamed of his not-so-impressive gang, a band of no-hopers and annoying boys who wouldn't shut up.

'Go on blue boy. Enlighten me.' He spat out the words, contemptuously. I was feeling a little faint but was attempting to be as daunting as the others. The power of this evil man was nothing now. I'd felt genuinely terrified by him and his short temper on the times we'd met — and he'd stolen my precious watch.

Seb must have noticed my discomfort.

'Captain. Some water for our attractive guest, if you please.' I appreciated his kindness. A part of the gallant man I thought I knew was there still.

Jesse brought his canteen from the saddle and I sipped it as Seb began to relate his theories.

'Firstly, should I call you Mad Charlie or simply Charlie? Not that it matters. You may be Little Miss Muffet for all I care. Your days as a thief and murderer are over. Your bunch of misfits were stealing money and passing most of it on to that banker, MacTavish. He'd been giving you information on the coach shipments and it was your job to steal them.'

'MacTavish? Never heard of him.' Charlie wasn't going to admit defeat easily.

'You must have. You see Charlie, there is no gold mine . . . never was. What I stole was a package of limestone addressed to the assay office. Archie Applegate was very close-lipped regarding the contents, yet he did let slip what they were to various people we suspected of being in collusion with you. Silver, zinc, copper, opals, even rubies. The person he mentioned gold to was your banker mate. MacTavish.'

Charlie sighed. He'd been caught out.

I remembered MacTavish mentioning gold to me at the dance but never suspected the significance. Gradually, I understood how elaborate Seb and Archie had been to root out the mastermind behind this New Eden project. I imagined that, armed with the information, Seb had enough evidence to arrest the banker on charges of working with the bushrangers and presumably plotting to cause some local insurrection.

Charlie looked up at us, his clothes and skin covered in dust from the explosion that had effectively disabled him. His sight and hearing were both back but whatever fight he'd had in him was gone.

'Alright, MacTavish passed us information but he's not alone, Midnight. I don't understand. What's all this to do with you? You're a bushranger, wanted in Tasmania and for murder here.'

Seb answered, 'I'll tell you all in good time, but one final question. Which one of you killed Reverend Cathcart at the Jerilderie church?'

There was a genuine look of shock in Charlie's eyes. 'What the . . . ? That was weeks ago. We got told he was too nosey and to do him in. He was a nobody. I killed him. Me. It was dead easy. He didn't have a gun or nothing and they paid me to do it. What's it to you anyway, Midnight?'

Seb tensed but did nothing physical. I could sense his outrage, though.

'He was a friend of mine, Michaels — a good friend who would make ten of your cronies. His death is the reason that I came here and brought this crack team of police officers with me.'

Charlie didn't understand. He continued to stare at Seb then searched the surroundings.

'Coppers? What coppers? I don't see no coppers here?'

Seb took off his hat then slowly his mask and hood as well, shaking his head to loosen the hair. The others, including Jesse, did the same. Charlie could hardly believe it!

'Charlie Michaels, I'm Detective First-Class Sebastian Longstreet of the New South Wales Criminal Investigation Bureau. You're all under arrest for murder, highway robbery and . . . well, the rest doesn't matter. You'll hang — and may the Lord have mercy on your souls because no one else will.'

Bert was awake and babbling now that he was innocent and that he'd recently joined the gang by mistake. Then he glared at me and spat our vindictive words that it was all my fault.

I turned away and walked off with Archie.

'Shall we go, Mr Applegate? I think I have had enough here.'

Archie had a few bruises on his face from his kidnapping but nothing serious. He watched as the three outlaws were pulled to their feet and slung over their horses before being tied on. The police were making certain they couldn't escape on the journey to jail.

Seb came over, his shoulders slumped from the stress of this successful operation. He made a point of not approaching me.

'We're returning to Jerilderie, Major,' Archie announced. 'The fourth gang-member is probably heading there too and will be telling all the others in this conspiracy that Midnight has caught Charlie's gang. I guess MacTavish still thinks he's safe but whatever plans the conspirators have will be thrown into disarray now that Charlie's not around to do their dirty work. When do you think you'll arrest the rest?'

'Monday, no doubt. I'll coordinate operations with the undercover team. If we hit all the seditionists at the same time, no one should be hurt. Sadly, we're still unsure of the identity of the shadowy mastermind but I'm certain MacTavish will tell us after his arrest. A pity we couldn't swoop on the whole lot at once. Then I can go home and leave this bloody place forever.'

Archie noted him glance at me, an unspoken disappointment between us. I felt dismayed despite the realisation that Charlie and Bert were no longer free to pillage and assault innocent people. Whatever Seb and I shared was gone, and I had no idea what had gone wrong.

12

The journey back from Wombat Ridge was almost leisurely. We were neither of us in a hurry. To be fair, neither were the horses. Jesse and I had pushed them hard in the frantic ride to get there in time to warn Seb that Charlie's gang were coming. The trap was sprung and three stinking rats were now on their way to jail and soon after to meet their maker.

I imagined that Archie had his issues to mull over. He'd put his faith in Seb and that had been rewarded. I'd done the same and . . . well, it hadn't.

It had been fine until he saw me in my male clothing, there, ready to help him capture the criminals. Was it my less than feminine attire or me simply not being the stay-at-home, cook-meals and caring-for-kiddies sort of perfect wifey that most men wanted in a marriage?

Not that we'd gotten that far as to discuss nuptials but any relationship between a bloke and a woman would lead down the aisle. Otherwise, there would be no point to falling in love, would there? I was nineteen for goodness sake, a woman in every sense of the word in a harsh land where the average life expectancy of a male was 40 and a female 42. I'd be lucky to see my grandchildren born. Most women had a half-dozen babies in the hope that two would live to adulthood. It was a sad fact that John Junior might be the third John Junior in that family, the father John constantly hoping that he'd have one son who'd survive to carry on his name.

'Quite a couple of weeks for you, Miss Stevens,' Archie commented as we trotted along.

'By the by, how are you finding your boarding with Mrs Huxley?'

Was this more than polite conversation? My answer prompted more searching questions of a personal nature, what did she enjoy, was her cooking acceptable and did she ever express regrets of loneliness at being a widow?

'Forgive my impertinence and bluntness, Mr Applegate. Are you . . . shall we say interested in courting the good widow?'

He turned so bright that I thought he would collapse from apoplexy, his skin the colour of the ripest strawberry I had ever beheld.

'Is it that obvious, Miss Stevens? I feel ashamed to have confessed that to you. Besides, what might such an accomplished lady find of attraction in an old codger like me?'

'You'd be surprised but you are asking the wrong person. I'm an innocent when it comes to the opposite gender as my experiences this day have demonstrated. Nevertheless, you would do well to inquire from Ma whether a picnic one Sunday arvo was possible. The worst she could say is 'No', and then you would at least have an answer. Yet if she were to acquiesce, your future may be together rather than apart.'

It was food for thought. We rode in contemplation for a time before he spoke.

'Miss Stevens? Grace. I didn't realise that you were privy to Seb's secrets until today. He's a fine man, putting his life on the line to unravel this dark conspiracy that has infected my town. May I ask . . . ?'

'Do I love him? I thought that I did. A young woman's fantasy. Too much Jane Austen.' Realising Archie had possibly not heard of my favourite authoress, I added a brief explanation.

'There is nothing amiss with love, dear Miss Stevens. Believe it or not, I have been there and may, God willing, find another to adore in my twilight years.'

He didn't mention a name though I was certain that he had my landlady in mind.

'A word of advice from an old man. Don't dismiss your feelings for the Detective nor his for you. If I were to suggest speaking to a close friend of his, the Reverend Peabody may shed some light on our secretive Major Midnight.'

I was surprised and not for the first time today.

'Reverend Peabody? Don't tell me he's in Seb's spy ring. I'm aware of Mr O'Shane and Ma of course. Is there anyone else hiding away under the pretence of subterfuge to uncover this New Eden conspiracy? Perhaps Mrs Hawkshaw's new-born babe or the blacksmith's dog?'

He grinned. 'Not that I've heard. Reverend Peabody was a friend of both our previous Reverend Cathcart and of Seb. From what I hear they were all in the seminary together, yet Seb chose a different path, to save people's mortal bodies while his two friends saved their souls. I gather they kept in close contact though. Seb told me that his dead friend wrote to him about what he suspected was happening here, on the day before Charlie murdered him.'

The spring sunshine was causing us to perspire a lot so we again stopped for a drink by a tributary of Billabong Creek. The horses drank from the stream while we used our canteens.

Although dusty with nary a breath of wind, the dry, brown landscape had a beauty to it that made me glad I'd chosen a life away from the soot-covered sterile city of my birth. A flock of galahs wheeled through the sky above us, settling like a white and pink blanket around the shores of the stream.

I could appreciate what attracted a certain group of people to come to the middle of nowhere. Life would be harsh yet they understood that. There was the raw excitement in this strange new land, a challenge to share with those of a like-minded constitution. Whatever their old life was, it could be cast aside for a fresh start. They could change their name, their occupation . . .

And me. What was I escaping from?

My family life had been wonderful but it was the expected conformity to the mores of a woman in Sydney that I was fleeing from, I guessed. Simply put, I was never going to be a social butterfly, behaving like all of the others there. As for riding astride a horse or even worse, bareback, it was so abhorrent to the side-saddle riders, they would never accept me in their upmarket circles.

'Goodness, Grace. Proper ladies would never do that. One has to consider one's prospects for marriage,' was what one of my fellow pupil teachers had told me before tossing me aside like ashes from the grate.

Would it matter to Seb? At this rate, I'd never find out unless we resolved whatever problems he had with me.

* * *

It was a good thing Archie knew the way back to Jerilderie. Even with a compass, I would have struggled, more likely to end up in Adelaide. If anyone were to ask, we'd not mention the aborted kidnapping or capture of Charlie's gang.

True, the fourth one who escaped, would be spreading the word to the conspirators but to the rest of Jerilderie, we'd gone for a long ride, Archie and I. At least, that was our story and we were sticking to it.

As we sighted and approached our

town, he thanked me for what I'd done but had one further bit of advice for me. It concerned Seb.

'Grace, I know that you and he have feelings for one another. Today things went wrong between you both and I pray that you work through that.

'I may have met Seb on but a few occasions but he came to help our town, not because he had to, but because he wanted to. There are a great number of emotions churning away inside him. A dark history filled with devils and demons that would crush someone like me.

'Don't dismiss him or his love because of what happened at Wombat Ridge. Please?'

I nodded. Already that ire I'd felt towards Seb had waned. He'd done a fine thing today despite his reaction to me. I owed it to him to discover more about Seb Longstreet and I knew exactly who to ask for advice.

★ ★ ★

245

I brought Ma Huxley up to date with the day's dramatic developments. It was right as she was a part of the inner circle. When asked if she'd heard of new gossip about the goings-on with this New Eden, she told me she'd heard nothing. That was apart from love being in the air, as Archie and I were seen riding together.

I chuckled and she joined in. Gossip. At least some things were the same as the Big Smoke.

Then she told me again that she was sweet on him herself but he'd never reciprocated. There was a note of regret in her voice. Two lonely people, afraid to declare what they felt. I wondered. Was I too inexperienced to be a match-maker? Because Seb and I had issues there was no reason to deny my two new friends some happiness.

As we sat, discussing anything that came to mind, I turned my questions towards Seb and her acquaintance with him in Bathurst. Perhaps she'd give me an insight into his unusual behaviour at Wombat Ridge. To me, it made no sense save that he disapproved of strong, independent women.

Recalling that afternoon of bliss we shared on the banks of the creek, I did not accept that he felt that way. Did he not ask me to take the bit between my teeth and kiss him rather than the other way around? He wanted me as an equal, surely — except when I arrived garbed as a man.

Then to compound it, I was the one to save us both from blabbermouth Bert as he held me as a shield. Had I not taken the initiative to disarm and knock Bert halfway into 1878, who could guess if either of us would be alive now?

Ma offered as much help as she was able to although it had been years since she'd seen him. As a young constable, he was keen, honest yet naive, convinced that right would always triumph over evil. Perchance that was from his seminarian upbringing, I thought.

'He was enthusiastic, I recall that. My hubby always said he'd go far and he has. Had a sister, a twin. Not identical of course, her being a girl but they looked alike. Only saw her the once, mind. She was bright as the sun on a clear, blue day. Rose . . . ? Yes, I believe she was Rose. Probably married with young'uns by now, I'll wager. I must ask how she is when he returns.'

I told her of our deduction that the criminal informant was Mr MacTavish, the banker. Ma was convinced he didn't have the brains to tie his shoelaces, let alone execute a detailed uprising to usurp the New South Wales government from the control of this part of the colony.

'Is there anyone rich or powerful enough to do that, then?'

She mused over the answer, apparently undecided. 'Mr Grenville Younger, that American you met at the dance. He's rich and owns a large sheep and wheat growing property. Doesn't come into town much, a bit of a recluse in his way.'

'But . . . ?'

Ma put down her knitting.

'But I can't believe he's involved or is the mastermind behind this. He's a patriot, loves this land, although he does resent the influence that Britain has on us. Throws a big party in town these past few years on July the fourth to celebrate his birthday. No, I don't believe he's the one Seb and the others are after, Grace. Maybe MacTavish is the one in charge?'

'Did you say the fourth of July was his birthday? That's too coincidental. It's also American Independence Day. The United States declared that they were no longer in the British Empire one hundred and one years ago in 1776.'

'Oh my,' Ma muttered as though she'd realised a point of significance she'd failed to mention.

'What is it, Ma?' I asked, a frisson of cold making me shiver in the balmy night.

'There was a wagon that had a loose wheel, stopped outside this house nigh on a month ago. The driver was very concerned about the load. We got to chatting as you do and I brought him a cuppa.

Said he was headed for Mr Younger's ranch, 'Little Georgia'. There was a tarpaulin over it but one tie was loose. I saw the boxes. Thought it said 'Dynamite' but it didn't. I'd seen the 'mite' letters printed. It said another word . . . here, I wrote it down because I didn't recognise it.'

Ma fished out a small booklet from her apron with a pencil attached and she quickly thumbed through the pages.

'Anyway, when I asked the driver, he said they were fireworks for a party. But what party? It's over nine months until July. Didn't make sense to me so that's why I wrote it — ah, here it is. Never did find out what it meant. Maybe you would recognise it? Jelly . . . ?'

I took the booklet, straining to read the light pencil markings in the flickering light from the lamps. 'The word's 'gelignite', Ma. It's an explosive more dangerous than dynamite, invented two years ago by a bloke called Noble in Sweden.'

Ma dropped her knitting and used

some very unladylike words — for which she immediately apologised.

'No need to ask for forgiveness,' I said having thought those same words myself. The crates were definitely not fireworks in any sense of the word.

Ma pondered on that disclosure, her teeth gritted together.

'We's got to let Seb know as soon as. There's no logical reason for a cockie such as Younger to have explosives . . .'

I finished her train of thought. 'Not unless he's planning a war.'

13

Was it happenstance that, of all the
people in Jerilderie, I would be one of
the few who understood what gelignite
was, apart from Mr Younger, of course?
Would Seb recognise it?

My father was renowned as Dynamite
Dan. After Mr Nobel, who had invented
dynamite, announced a more stable
form of explosive, gelignite, not two
years since, we had discussed changing
Papa's moniker to Gelignite Dan, even
though it meant no elegant alliteration.
In the end, he decided against it. 'I'm
was too old to reinvent myself, Grace.
I'll stay Dynamite Dan until I die. I owe
it to my followers.'

If Papa heard that I'd discovered a
clue to this conspiracy because of that
discussion, he would call it 'serendipity'.
Me, I didn't believe in luck. Nevertheless, I would mention it to the Reverend
Peabody at church tomorrow. He might

have a way to contact Seb somehow through the telegraph, using a secret code so as not to alert the conspirators.

I wished to speak to him regarding Seb in any case. He might be able to explain Seb's irritation with me earlier this day.

* * *

Ma and I arrived at church too late for me to say little more than Good Morning to the Reverend. Others were arriving to take their places inside. The day, as was usually the case, was sunny and dry. Oh — and let us not forget the flies that made their presence felt, attracted by the salt in our perspiration, I'd heard. In their way, they were as irritating today as Bert had been yesterday. No wonder I'd lost my rag with him. My hand ached every time I flexed my fingers.

I managed a quick word with the beaming Reverend to ask if we could chat after the service. He'd agreed politely.

He spoke of many things in his sermon, including right and wrong and the grey areas in between. Then he gave an uplifting speech on the beauties of nature which we took for granted: the first smile of a baby, the sight of those first shoots in a cockie's field after much welcome rain, the colours of the morning skies as the golden sun rose above the horizon.

'Most of you realise that the Morning Star and the Evening Star are the same, appearing at different times during the year. However, it is not a star but a planet, Venus, the closest planet in the vast Heavens to our own.'

His voice was measured, a far cry from the monotonous droning of many church services in my past.

'As I said, last week, appearances can be deceiving. If the Devil had appeared in the Garden of Eden, dressed not as a serpent but as a cute koala, would he be any less evil?'

That caused a wave of laughter and smiles, though not, I noted as I looked around, with Mr Younger and his ranch-hands. Since he'd mentioned Eden, I wondered if it were a deliberate ploy to upset the conspirators.

The Reverend paused, removed his glasses and mopped his bald head as he waited for silence again.

'No, my children. The Devil is the Devil, although he was once an Angel. Do not be taken in by his lies spoken with a forked tongue, even if he appears to be your best friend. Listen by all means, but you are not mindless sheep. You are aware of evil and righteousness. You must decide which path your heart and your mind tells you to take.'

We all felt joyful as we left the church, Reverend Peabody clasping hands in his as he bade each person or family farewell. He spoke to each child as he did so until he and I remained alone.

'Grace Stevens. You wished to speak with me. How are you, my child? Shall we adjourn to the sacristy, such as it is? Barely room to swing a kitten. However, it is private and should suffice.'

I followed him in but had hardly begun when there was a loud rap on the closed door.

Chester Peabody scowled slightly. 'I'll just be a moment, Miss Stevens. Bear with me. I'm not expecting anyone.' As he opened the portal, I could see a farm-hand on the threshold, holding his hat in his hands.

'Begging your pardon, Reverend . . . ma'am. Mr Younger has requested the presence of both of you for Sunday lunch. If you'd come with me, we'd best get a wriggle on. He likes to start at noon precisely.' The bloke gave a cursory smile, stepping back as if he were expecting us to follow.

'Today for lunch, my good chap? That is extremely kind of Mr Younger although I'm afraid I have other plans.'

The Reverend faced me so I added, 'Me too. Mrs Huxley at the boarding house is expecting me. Perhaps next Sunday?'

'Mr Younger was most insistent. Had a sheep killed just this morning. Besides I have taken the liberty of telling your landlady of the change of plans. He is very keen to make you both welcome and apologises for the brief notice. His chef is Italian and does put on a mighty fine spread according to other guests he's had in the past. Mr Appleby and Mrs Schneider are already on their way in the other buckboard.'

Although I was far from pleased at the rudeness of assuming that we were at his beck and call like servants, the fact that we were not the only guests allayed my anger somewhat. In retrospect, I must have had a sign painted on my forehead with the words 'gullible, guileless idiot' in tiny writing.

Seb would be pleased with me if I brought back intelligence on this Mr Younger character, so I nodded. The Reverend chose to follow my lead, perhaps feeling he should be protective or sensing that what I wished to discuss was urgent, at least to me.

'Fine. We'll come. Please allow me to change into some more comfortable clothing. These raiments are hardly suitable for travel or a meal.'

The bloke interrupted with that same

Cheshire Cat grin. 'No need, Reverend. The boss requested you wear your church robes. You see, he had his chapel, fresh built next to the house and would greatly appreciate your advice and your blessing. Shall we go, please?'

Talk about cracking the whip! This bloke was being pushy. Grudgingly I stood to leave and followed the two of them outside. While a buckboard wasn't the comfiest way to get from A to B, we had no choice. The driver unfolded a blanket to place on the dirty seat and helped me to climb up in a fashion which didn't display too many of my petticoats. I fastened my bonnet.

'Don't worry, Miss Stevens,' whispered Chester Peabody. 'If there are problems, I'll look out for you.'

It wasn't that reassuring as the Reverend struck me as a bloke who wouldn't say boo to a stuffed goose. He'd be watching out for me but who would be keeping an eye on him?

It was a dusty, warm and most uncomfortable. Cobb and Co was decadent luxury by comparison. With the driver and two of us on the seat and second employee of Little Georgia lying behind us, it was cramped. At least the buckboard acted as protection from the horses' rear hooves if they bucked. I already had enough aches and bruises from Saturday's shenanigans to last me a lifetime.

The trip wasn't picturesque either. After all, one gum tree pretty-much resembles every other one. The countryside vegetation was in that twilight time of the year, as it altered from the verdant green of spring rains to the colour of dust and desiccation. Rabbits flittered everywhere, the ground almost alive with their numbers.

'How large is Mr Younger's property?' Chester asked before almost choking on a fly before he spat it out.

'Around three thousand acres at present but he's planning on expanding a lot. A bloody lot,' the driver replied before he and his companion burst out in horselaughs, treating it as a joke to which we were not privy.

We passed a fence and gate with a sign naming his domain, a man standing by the gate posts with a rifle.

'Roos,' the driver answered when I asked him the reason. 'Dumb animals can't read the No Trespassing signs.' Despite knowing that they were pests to some people, I doubted that the guard was there simply to shoot roos.

Given the size of Little Georgia, it was some time before we arrived at the sprawling homestead replete with out-buildings. We'd been beside a line of telegraph poles for ages, surprising to see, as this was private land. Could it be that Grenville needed his private com-munication post? What for? The stock exchange in Sydney made sense but it was unlikely.

As we gratefully alighted from the buckboard, I could see the sagging lines terminating at a large shed some two hundred yards from the house. Curi-ouser and curiouser, as Alice had mused in Wonderland.

The yard was bustling with activity, men with broad-rimmed hats loading and unloading wagons and herding horses in the extensive corrals. It was striking. There were no women visible which was a little disconcerting. However, Frau Schneider was here, presumably awaiting us inside.

Entering the home, we were greeted by a Chinese woman who offered us cool drinks and directed us to rooms where we could freshen up.

French labelled soap was by the basin of clean water, and a soft, plush towel. At last I felt human, dabbing the soft cotton against my cheeks. I retied the bows in my hair, smoothed down my dress and took a deep breath.

Into the lion's den.

The young lady guided me into the ornately decorated dining room. Although the Reverend was seated, there was no sign of Archie or the manageress of the hotel after all. We were the sole guests. Chester raised a quizzical eyebrow yet said nothing. He must have felt as puzzled as I, by their absence.

Almost immediately, Grenville Younger strode in, his boots reverberating on the polished floorboards. No carpet? Then I examined the room in more detail. Elaborate plasterwork on the ceilings and walls yet no signs of a woman's touch. It was almost antiseptically sterile in its austerity.

The Chinese woman came in with two more kitchen staff, wordlessly dishing our food onto what looked like pure silver plates. Once finished, they bowed and withdrew. It was totally over the top, and evidence that he was intent on demonstrating his power and affluence. The few words spoken to his staff were dismissive insults when the girl spilt some mint sauce on the pristine white linen table cloth. I saw her cringe.

'Greetings Miss Stevens, Reverend Peabody. Or should I say 'Howdy'? Have to remember my roots.' He smiled with his lips, his eyes remaining impassive and cold. 'Thank you for accepting my invitation. Would you say grace, please,

Reverend? I'm famished.'

I felt like interjecting that we'd come only becuase we had little choice. Papa's words to bide my time sprang to mind.

'Shouldn't we wait for the others? Mrs Schneider and Mr Applegate?' I asked politely.

'Oh them? A communication breakdown with my staff. It's just you two and me. I'm keen to find out all about you. Especially you, my adorable Miss Stevens. You are an extremely fetching woman, indeed.' He faced the Reverend. 'Our meal is becoming cold. Say grace, Reverend? Now, if you please.'

To be honest, the meal was quite affable and delicious, although it was evident that our host did not sanction any disagreements with his 'requests'.

We discussed our respective life stories, mine being rather brief given that I'd yet to do anything. My father was mentioned in passing. Grenville, for that was the name he insisted we call him, was not aware of my father's fame and that suited me.

I was surprised that his sons, the Twee-dle Twins were not here with their father. Was all not well in Wonderland? Then I recalled that they were not close but that he'd hoped that they would return to the fold.

We were playing a game, I suspected, as each of us was circumspect in disclosing too much information. If Younger were the conspiracy leader then the surviving member of Charlie's gang must have informed him regarding the fate of his pet thief.

Once the meal concluded, I broached the subject of our return to Jerilderie. For my part, I had preparations for Monday's lessons to attend to. I thanked Mr Younger for his wonderful hospitality, complementing him of the quality and quantity of our lunch.

'Returning is unfortunately out of the question, Miss Stevens.'

I felt that chill in my bones again. 'Are we prisoners?' I inquired, quite alarmed.

'Prisoners? Here in Little Georgia? Goodness gracious me! What sort of

264

host do you believe me to be, Miss Stevens? Do I appear to be some dastardly villain from a cheap dime novel?'

I assumed it was a rhetorical question as my answer would have been less than flattering.

'No,' he said, standing, 'I wanted you to see my chapel first. An indulgence for me to have your approval and your blessing, Reverend? After that, my men will return you to your respective homes.'

Fair enough, I thought.

A few more minutes only, and then we could leave and hopefully my skin would cease to crawl.

The chapel was stunning; large enough for thirty to sit on the pews and admire the marble altar and elaborate stained glass windows in their Heavenly splendour.

'It's an indulgence,' Grenville Younger admitted. 'But it will be the perfect venue for my imminent nuptials.'

That was a surprise and we both congratulated him. The Reverend gave the building a form of blessing, not that I understood how such a chapel was consecrated or even if Mr Younger were the same denomination as us. Nevertheless, once it had finished, I breathed a quiet sigh of relief. We would soon be on our way from this oppressive mausoleum of a home.

There was an interruption as one of Grenville's sons entered wearing his police uniform. It was evident that they had resolved whatever differences they'd had.

Grenville took him to one side to discuss the trooper's news. I strained to hear their hushed conversation while Chester wandered closer to the window, his head tipped back as he stared upwards. He was studying the very detailed but hard to visualise theme with the leaded glass being in such tiny fragments.

While it was hard to eavesdrop, I did catch keywords and the gist of their exchange. The younger Younger was telling his father that the banker MacTavish had disappeared from his home along with other names I vaguely recognised.

That surprised me as it was Sunday and I was certain that the swoop by police was to be on Monday.

Grenville was concerned although not overly so. It might be a temporary setback in the plans but not a great cause for concern. It seemed whatever roles they had played in Grenville's machinations were complete.

'Any idea who took them, Elmer?' the silver-haired American demanded.

'Midnight and his gang. They were seen riding off from Dawson's farm this afternoon. Dawson was tied up.'

That didn't sound right. Seb couldn't be back from Wagga.

Grenville rubbed his chin, those thick black eyebrows meeting in the middle like two hairy caterpillars.

'Midnight again. Damn. Why would a bushranger be bothered with them? Unless he's not what he seems. Ask the telegraph operator to send messages to Sydney and the other capitals. See what you can discover about this interfering so-and-so. In the meantime, double the guards and make certain that the telegraph is working properly. I'll give the order first thing Tuesday.'

I noted Chester still attempting to make sense of the glass window, finally moving towards the opposite end to give him a distant view. Perhaps, like some impressionist paintings, the dots of colour were best viewed from afar.

'Why not tomorrow, Daddy?' Herman inquired.

'Because tomorrow's my wedding day, you idiot.' From the expression on the youth's face, it was not the first time this particular insult had been levelled at him.

Meanwhile, Chester was beckoning me to where he was. He was frantic enough to suggest it was more crucial than any further titbits to overhear. I wandered over, perplexed what the big attraction was.

'Try squinting your eyes a little and look, Miss Stevens. That window.' I was annoyed but did as requested. The jumbled chunks of colours merged to a scene of two naked people, a man and a woman, in a jungle. Leaves discretely covered their unmentionable parts.

'What?' I asked Chester.

'The Garden of Eden,' he whispered in my ear and I gasped. Grenville Younger was the mastermind after all. No doubt.

We had to leave and tell Seb. Grenville had dismissed his son and came to join us in that leisurely way that denoted a king inspecting his kingdom.

'Magnificent, isn't it? Our Lord's dream of perfection.'

We agreed, effusing over the spectacular image with the afternoon sun shining through. The church was awash with a rainbow of light.

'However, we really must be leaving now, Mr Younger. Thank you for your hospitality. You said we could go now.'

He fixed me with those intense eyes of his and grinned. 'Unfortunately for you, I lied, Miss Stevens. You and the Reverend will be needed tomorrow at the finest wedding you will ever see.'

Needed. What to prepare or serve

food? Surely not. Then why? Then I had a terrible vision.

'This wedding, Mr Younger. Who is the lucky bride-to-be? Perhaps I know her?'

'Oh, I should think you do, Grace Stevens. My gorgeous bride, the woman with whom I shall spend my future life and who will bring forth a new generation of the Younger dynasty? Of course, she will be you.'

14

My nightmare was just beginning. 'You can't be serious. Why would I marry you? We don't even know one another, I do not love you and you're old enough to be my father. The very idea is quite disgusting!'

Grenville Younger remained emotionless, his contempt for my opinion disdainfully eerie.

'You will marry me and the good Reverend will perform the ceremony otherwise I shall kill everyone you are close to in front of your eyes.'

This was unbelievable! The time for polite decorum was done. I lashed out vehemently.

'You won't get away with this, even if I do give in to your insane demands. You can't flout the law like this. Kidnapping . . . extortion . . . You'll be jailed for this you — you monster.'

The way he scoffed was a new type of

frightening. His American accent that added to the quiet arrogance of this man was too much. Worse still, we had no chance of escape. No chance at all.

'In a day or two, I will be the law. Judge, jury, and executioner if need be. My dream of an independent country in the heart of this continent will be a reality. New Eden. The foreigners scorned by your English controlled puppet governments will flock here in their tens of thousands, ready to defend us against all invaders. Criminals will choose us as a haven even as they rob and plunder the surrounding colonies. We will be an oasis of new hope in this continent.'

The truth was out. We were dealing with a seriously deranged megalomaniac. Whether this 'dream' of his would succeed, was immaterial. Innocent people would be hurt.

I heard a noise behind Chester and me. Two armed men had arrived.

Younger waved his hand dismissively before turning to face his altar. He was done talking.

'Take them away and lock them in the cells. Our guests need to contemplate their futures and get a good night's sleep for tomorrow.'

A decent sleep would not be possible, I decided upon inspecting the accommodation of adjoining rooms in which we were placed. They were jail cells with heavy barred doors and walls of cold, hard stone. The cells in Jerilderie were of wood, sufficiently sturdy to keep most prisoners from escaping. These cells were another indication of Younger's plans and paranoia.

The wooden bed had a thin lumpy mattress and nothing else. The setting sun's rays through the barred window gave a rosy glow making this part of hell bleaker still. The prison, for that was what it was, occupied a structure well away from the palatial homestead.

We'd passed a bunkhouse for the twenty or so farmhands who doubled as Younger's private army. The telegraph station was visible through the window. If we could get there, we could send a message for help but we neither of us were familiar with Morse Code.

Trying to take my mind off tomorrow's fiasco of a marriage — and, worse still, the wedding night — I asked Chester about Seb.

Having explained what had transpired at Wombat Ridge and Seb's reaction to me, he spoke to me from the cell to my right. We couldn't see one another but we could talk. At least I wasn't alone.

'How were you dressed, exactly?' Chester asked. That was a puzzle. He'd been Seb's friend for years. Why should my attire be of concern? Nevertheless, I told him.

He sighed, audibly. 'That explains why he was shocked, Grace.' He paused long enough for me to prompt him.

'Seb had a sister, Rose. They were very close. Rose was a, I believe the word is 'tomboy'. She always dressed as a boy, had short hair too. Hated wearing dresses. Perhaps the sight of you in similar attire, your hair piled under your hat ... She was pretty like you, pale

274

complexion and a cheeky elfin face. He called her 'pixie'. It suited her; mischievous, always getting into trouble and fights. Naturally, Seb was there to help her out. He was the strong one.'

I considered what Chester and Ma had told me of this Rose. I would love to meet her. We would have a lot in common. Then I paused.

'Sorry, Reverend. Did you say *had* a sister?'

'Yes. She was killed. He was there. In Bathurst. He was a detective sent to a siege at a bank. Rose was a teller there, always joking with the customers and very popular. The robbers used her as a shield but, faced with a dozen armed police awaiting them as they exited the bank, Rose was shot by one of the thieves. Seb saw it all. It devastated him.'

I began to sob, our dire predicament paling before Seb's loss. I hadn't realised. No wonder seeing me, dressed like that then being accosted by that worm, Bert. The emotions must have been overwhelming for Seb. I couldn't wait to see him again to hold and comfort him though that prospect was, at the moment, slim indeed.

As the sun rapidly vanished and twilight enveloped the cell, I sat despondently on the edge of my bunk bed. A plaything for his Lordship. Was this my life to come?

Even Chester's words of promise that all was not lost, failed to assuage the bleakness. Not even a last meal for the condemned woman, it seemed as night was upon us in all its shadow-filled finality. I sat there trying to decide what our options were. It was probable that no one suspected where we were. That story, telling Ma Huxley we were having lunch with Younger? Yet another untruth.

There was a noise outside. Was help on its way? I stopped breathing and listened.

Men were talking, coming closer. A door opened and closed, a lantern's light flickering as footsteps approached our cells.

'I brought you some food,' one of the Younger boys said. There's an opening on the bottom of the cell door. I'll pass them through. Ladies first.'

In spite of the way I felt about the corrupt policeman, I thanked him for his consideration. There was a small oil lamp on the tray that he lit before passing it through. I knelt to retrieve it, surprised to see a watch secreted under a napkin.

I stood in front of the cell grate at eye level, staring at his face in shock. 'But that's my —' I began before he hushed me. He leant forward as did I, our heads both touching the rigid bars of cold metal.

'Seb retrieved it from Charlie. Said you'd want it back.' His whisper was low because of the guard at the cellblock door.

I didn't respond. It was some sort of trap. Elmer was not to be trusted.

He smirked. 'Seb mentioned you'd be cagey.

That's why he gave me the watch. Also told me to say he's sorry for his behaviour at Wombat Ridge. Said something about cloud watching too. Me and my brother are working with Major Midnight, undercover like.'

'But your father. He's running the show.'

Elmer explained quickly and quietly. 'Me and Herman haven't bothered with Daddy for years. He killed our mum when we were teenagers. Just a few days ago he approached us to make amends; restore his dynasty, he says. I weren't interested but Herman told me to hear him out. Good thing, too. Told us all about his crazy scheme.'

'Hurry up in there, mate,' someone yelled from outside.

Elmer cast a sideways glance towards where he came from. 'Keep your pants on, Nate. What's the rush?' he shouted before returning to whispering.

'We plays along with him for appearance's sake but telegraphed Sydney police from well aways from here. Then Seb turns up at the station, told us who he is and asks us to spy. Honest, Miss Stevens. We's had no idea he has all them guns and explosives until today.'

'Hey, Elmer,' the guard shouted. 'What's taking you so long?'

The trooper told me, 'Start screaming at me, Miss. Loud and nasty as you can.'

I started to yell with all the venom I could muster just as the door opened.

'Just coming, Nate,' Elmer shouted over me. 'The stupid sheila here is trying to con me into letting her go by taking her clothes off. So I let her. Just told her Daddy's the only one with the keys. She's not happy.' He laughed.

Nate joined in. 'She won't get out any other way. The boss built this jail to be impregnable.' Naturally, the guard tried to see me but couldn't as I'd moved to the side of the grill. He stormed off in a huff.

Elmer waited a sec before finishing.

'Seb's coming for you, Miss Stevens. Just do everything he says no matter how silly. It's the only way we'll escape in one piece. We — me and Herman — have done some bad things but we're loyal to New South Wales. We have to stop our father.'

He gave Chester his meal then hurried out. I assumed Chester had heard enough to follow what had been said.

Once all was quiet, I asked him, 'If old man Younger has the sole key, how can Seb break us out?'

'Don't worry, Grace. He's as wily as a dingo, is Seb. Best eat up and get some shut-eye. If I'm correct, nothing will happen until everything's settled for the night.'

I smiled. Seb was coming for us. When would my bushranger lover make his move?

Midnight, of course.

* * *

I was dozing when a silhouetted shape at the window roused me.

'Wake up, Grace. Turn your bed over and crouch behind it in the far corner.'

It was Seb's voice. My heart filled with hope.

'But why?' I demanded, my speech soft for fear of alerting the guard.

'What did Elmer tell you? Simply do as I say, my love. Please.'

Hurriedly, I did as he asked while he did the same through Chester's cell window.

'Stay there. I'm blowing the wall apart.'

My eyes opened wide as I hugged the mattress to me, covering my ears and praying. The bed's solid wooden base had better be strong enough to save me. The seconds ticked by but I dare not raise my head. Then the room shook as the stones and mortar flew in all directions. A gaping hole allowed the cool, night air to gust in along with choking dust.

'Come on,' Seb yelled to us both. There was little point in being subtle any longer. He grabbed my hand, pulling me closer to kiss me.

Our Reverend emerged too.

'So much for the impregnable jail,' Chester observed as more rocks tumbled down at our feet. We made to run but three men appeared with six-guns levelled at us. The full moon made it easy for them to see us although Seb's lantern didn't help.

'Hold up, you lot or we shoot. Drop your gun, you.' It was the guard from earlier, pleased that he'd caught us. 'Crickey. Who have we got?' he said, lifting his lantern to illuminate Seb's masked face. 'Well, knock me down and call me a platypus. If it isn't Major Midnight hisself. I reckon Mr Younger will have quite a few words to say to you for wrecking his brand-new jail. And none of them will be pleasant.'

15

Well, so much for that escape. What had Seb been thinking, waking the entire compound of armed farmhands with this loud noise? The anger faded rapidly when I remembered what Elmer Younger had insisted . . . *Trust Seb. He knows what he's doing.*

As we were led off to face the music, Seb took my hand in his own gloved one, bending to whisper in my ear that he loved me. Three simple words that thrilled me despite the dilemma we were in.

'I love you too,' I replied.

'Hey, you two. Stop whispering,' my less-than-favourite guard shouted.

'What are you going to do about it?' I retorted. 'Shoot your boss's intended wife? I can see that do wonders for your prospects.'

'Er . . . alright You can talk — but no touching,' he conceded more quietly.

'About Wombat Ridge . . .' Seb began.

'It's forgotten. I can take care of myself . . . well usually. That jail was a problem. Thank you for trying to save me.'

He laughed. 'Oh, that wasn't the escape plan, Grace. As our Reverend preached, last week, impressions can be deceptive. If we're going to get through this, I'll need that splendid right hook of yours again.'

* * *

It was almost amusing that we all were told to wipe our feet as we entered Younger's home.

Like cattle, we were prodded and herded into a sumptuous living area that we'd not seen on our earlier, more cordial visit.

Grenville Younger was there, seated like a king upon a thrown, garbed in a silk dressing gown. There was a strange device on a table at his side with wires running to and through the window

284

frame. I'd seen telegraph keys yet this was different, a black bottomless cup fixed side on to a mounting and coil of copper wire.

My future husband was not pleased.

However, on seeing the single crown insignia on Major Midnight's sleeve, that anger was replaced with a gleeful smirk.

'Well done, lads. You caught the verminous beast who has been disrupting my plans. But firstly, let us see who you really are.' With a wave of his hand Younger indicated that the Major's hat, hood and mask should be removed by one of his minions.

Seb stood there, unmasked yet defiant. His height over the other blokes gave him an imposing air. Grenville Younger sensed it also though he pretended to be unperturbed.

'Why isn't he hand-cuffed?' he demanded. Our American friend's eyes betrayed him in his barked order. There was fear there.

'Who are you? I've seen you somewhere . . . ah, yes, the dance. A common

285

labourer.'

A series of shots sounded from the yard outside. A pause, then more. Although I was puzzled and not a little concerned, Younger remained outwardly calm, flexing his fingers, his legs folded as he watched Seb being restrained.

Moments later, Elmer Younger dashed in, a little out of breath.

'Well?' his father said,

'We shot the others in his gang, Daddy. All three. Do you want their bodies brought in?'

'Gracious no. All that blood on my rugs. Just leave them and tell the lads to stand down and get some kip. All of his gang are accounted for. We can move forward with the formation of New Eden Tuesday.'

Seb seemed to lose his dispassionate stance at that point.

'You monster!' he raged, making a move to attack the power-crazed land-owner.

He was reined back by the guards.

'Temper, temper, Major, although

I suspect you are not a Major after all, simply some want-to-be petty criminal with delusions of grandeur.'

'What? Like you?' Seb retorted.

Grenville sneered at that before regaining his composure. 'Tie him to a chair, then you two can leave. Get your sleep. Well done. As for you . . . Nate is it?' The guard nodded, pleased that his boss knew his name. 'You remain, Nate, in case Midnight becomes . . . quarrel-some.'

'Do you want the other two tied?' Nate inquired, indicating the Reverend and me.

'Hardly. An old man and a weakling girl? Just keep an eye on the bushranger.'

He faced Seb again, deciding to stand and glower down at him. 'As for me, Major. I'm no petty criminal. In a few days, I will be President of New Eden with this wench as my wife. My king-dom, free from the shackles of England and its draconian ways. We have guns and armaments enough to protect our independent land from the so-called authorities in Melbourne and Sydney. Gatling guns, field artillery, grenades, explosives by the ton, repeater rifles. We have them all — including a Winan's Steam Gun. And we have agents in the colonies' capitals, ready to act to destabilise the governments there. Our success is assured.'

'And how do you intend to contact these agents of yours, Younger?' Seb asked, that rage now replaced by a self-assuredness that indicated things were set to alter in this exchange of words.

'With this miracle device.' He indicated the black cup-like apparatus. 'Mr Bell, an American like myself, invented this device which carries my voice to a room hundreds of yards away. It will be the future. It is a telephonic device.'

I was astounded. Despite my hatred for him, I blurted out, 'You can talk to people far away, without shouting? That is unbelievable! There will be no need for Morse Code or the telegraph.'

'This one is for me to converse with my Morse operator in my Telegraph Office.

On Tuesday morn, I shall sit here, lift my telephonic apparatus and call him to initiate messages being sent everywhere. When my agents hear my command to action, they will carry out their tasks. Mainly sabotage, but an assassination or two.'

'What is the command?' Chester said.

'Why 'Genesis', of course, Reverend. Quite appropriate, don't you think?'

It was a rhetorical question, but Grenville Younger was extremely enamoured with his choice of words.

Then he stopped beaming and stared at Seb, intently watching the grandfather clock by the stone fireplace.

By now, it was almost a quarter to one in the morning. I was extremely tired but had to stay alert. Seb was handcuffed and tied to a chair. With the best intentions in the world, Chester was incapable of little else in a fight than preaching a man to death. Therefore, I'd be needed. When or how I did not understand.

There was one armed guard and Grenville himself, also armed. His gun was by his side on the same table as the device.

A puzzled expression came over him. 'Tell me, Midnight. What is the attraction with the time?'

'Depends. Is your clock accurate?'

Grenville Younger strode over to the timepiece. Was he suspecting a timed explosive to be secreted there? Satisfied that there was none he answered that yes, it was accurate.

Seb asked him. 'Why not show us that this miracle machine works? I mean, a device that carries voices over wires? You have to admit it sounds like the delusions of a lunatic. Give your telegraph operator a call. None of us are going anywhere in a hurry.'

Grenville was perplexed yet intrigued.

'Perhaps I will. The last bequest to a man soon to die . . . Major.'

He sat in his comfortable chair, lifted the object and put the black cup to his mouth.

'Hello. Hello. Are you hearing me, Mister Fabrini?' The long pause which followed irritated my prospective husband.

As if he were expecting it, Seb yawned and shrugged his shoulders indifferently.

'Mr Fabrini. Answer me.' Presumably, the operator was on duty all the time in the telegraph shed — or should have been.

Then a tinny voice responded. We all jumped. If we had been at a seance and a phantom had spoken from the netherworld we would not have believed it any less.

'Fabrini's taking a nap. It's The Captain here. Lovely set up you have, Mr Younger.'

'The Captain? I employ no Captain.' Younger and the guard were the ones who weren't grinning. Was this Seb's plan?

'I work with Major Midnight. We've been busy notifying the authorities in police stations everywhere to arrange dawn raids on all your highly placed accomplices. We have names, addresses and proof they are saboteurs and seditionists. Your New Eden will never happen.'

Younger ground his teeth audibly.

'Nate. Rouse the lads. My traitorous son has lied to me!'

I couldn't resist defending Elmer's actions. 'Lying? Learnt that from you, then.'

After the American snarled at me, he returned his attention to the telephone. He threw it to the floor, shattering it into fragments.

Nate started to move but hesitated. 'What about you, boss? I can't leave you alone with these three.'

Grenville Younger reached for his gun. 'They won't be a problem, Nate. Quickly — the lads. And this time kill them all, and bring Elmer and Herman to me.'

From outside there was a flash of bright light and a loud bang. More followed, with men screaming. Younger and Nate went to the windows, pulling the curtains aside.

'It's the bunkhouse, boss.'

Seb, Chester and I had a grand view too. Men attired in nightwear or long johns were streaming out blinded by the magnesium flares Seb's colleagues had lobbed inside. Those 'flash, bang, wallop' explosives certainly did a grand job of disorienting people.

The employees of Younger had hands to ears from the deafening noises. They were helpless in the face of the blue garbed men who pounced on them, disarmed them, then snapped restraints on their wrists and ankles. It was clear there were more than the three of Seb's gang than we believed were around.

Seb, tied to his chair, kicked out at me, indicating that Chester and I should take cover. There were more fun and games to come. The Reverend and I managed to duck behind some heavy settees just in time. The room lit up with a blinking flash, far greater than the ones used so far. Next second, the house was almost lifted off its foundations as a tremendous blast shattered the windows all around. Others explosions followed, flames and belching black clouds pouring from the remnants of the large shed. It had once housed Younger's arsenal of weapons and armaments. No longer.

'Noooo!' screamed the American, rushing past us to behold his dream quite literally going up in smoke.

More aftershocks shook the house. I assumed that no one was in the ammunition dump, it being on the other side of the house to the bunkhouse, telegraph hut, corrals and stables. Nate ran by too but was tripped by Seb who then threw himself forcefully onto the startled guard. His gun flew to the side. Grenville was distracted, having a conniption fit at the destruction of his dream!

From the floor wrestling with Nate, Seb yelled out, 'Your turn, Grace — do us proud!'

I was ready. Scrambling to my feet, I approached Grenville Younger from the back. His gun was held loosely in his hand. His anger was directed at the ongoing explosive display of fire, sparks and exploding shells lighting up the night sky with the most spectacular firework display I'd ever seen.

I yanked the gun from his hand before he could react, tossing it to Chester who'd gathered the other weapons already.

'You witch!' he growled, going for me like some demented bull at a matador.

I side-stepped nimbly, striking him in the solar plexus as he eyed me, saliva falling from his clenched lips.

'That's for kidnapping and locking us up!' I yelled, adrenalin pumping through my body. He doubled over as I let loose with a haymaker to his chin. 'And that's for trying to marry me!'

I was sure he didn't hear it as his feet left the floor, his body curving backwards until it crashed to the ground. He didn't get up.

I panted until I could slow my breathing. Seb was lying on top of Nate, the weight on him and the chair pinning the guard so effectively, he'd given up struggling.

'Remind me not to try marrying you against your will!' Seb laughed and I joined in.

Outside there was still the sound of

popping ammunition going off. Grenville's New Eden dream was a shattered ruin. I felt very elated and relieved.

'Everything alright?' Jesse asked as he entered with the two Younger lads.

They stared at their father, still on the floor but slowly coming around.

Jesse freed Seb then restrained Nate.

'Any regrets?' Seb wondered as he addressed the two sons, showing some sensitivity to the situation. In this Eden, it wasn't one brother killing the other but two brothers betraying their father.

'One,' said Herman, contemptuously. 'We should have stood up to this bully and murderer long ago.'

'You'll hang for this, 'Daddy', and we'll be there to watch it and later to dance on your grave.'

Elmer raised his foot but thought better of it. 'No. You're not worth it. Suffice it to say, 'Daddy Dearest', we shall inherit this property of yours and make it something great for the community. Provided we don't end up in jail for ignoring Charlie and his bushranging?'

It was a question he directed to Seb who told him that they wouldn't. The detailed sketches of New Georgia and the contents of the outbuildings had enabled Seb and Jesse's team of workers from the bridge to capture all of Younger's men without a single causality. Following that, they'd dynamited the weapons and munitions store. There was no question concerning the troopers' loyalty to New South Wales and to Australia in general.

Finally, it was decided we should all bed down for the night. No one would be leaving until the morning.

'On behalf of our father might we suggest the guest rooms in the house. We apologise for any dust or broken glass but the beds will be comfortable and the breakfast the best that Daddy's money can buy.'

Gallantly, I was offered the best and least damaged room in the house. Grenville was herded outside to join his henchmen who would be sleeping on the yard under guard.

Seb was in the room at the far end of the hall. We said good night although it was after two in the morning.

I asked Seb how he'd known that Chester and I were being held captive here.

He told me that they'd camped out on Saturday night with Charlie and the prisoners near a telegraph line. When he contacted Sydney, they'd passed on the Younger brothers' message about their father and New Eden.

He'd ridden back to Jerilderie asking the others to follow once the prisoners were handed over. Going to Ma's, he'd learnt of the gelignite and that I was missing. Elmer made enquiries and found me so they'd devised a way to rescue us.

I was so grateful that he'd come in time.

'You risked your life to save mine, Major Midnight. At any time that elaborate plan could have backfired and you may have died. That deserves a thank you kiss for starters.'

298

He obliged passionately, ever the gentleman. It felt so wonderful to have his broad, muscular arms around me, holding me so closely I could feel every breath he took.

Eventually, we parted though our hands remained on one another's shoulders.

'For starters?' he whispered, staring into my eyes intently in the dim lights of the hallway. Reaching up he stroked my hair before kissing my temple over and over.

I pushed him back enough so that we could see one another up close.

'Earlier tonight I was in a jail cell with thoughts of a forced marriage to a man I detested. He would have had his way with me and I would have been helpless to object.' The light of the oil lamp flickered as a reflection in his eyes. 'You must return to Sydney, your work in Jerilderie is done while I must remain for the children. But at this moment, my dearest Major Midnight, I want you with me in my bedroom.'

Was it too forward of me? I did not care. This was my chance of happiness though it was for a scant few hours.

I took his hand in mine to open the door.

He paused. 'Just one thing, Major Midnight is no longer, Grace. It's me, Seb. The Major will never ride again.'

'Do not say 'never', Seb. I've taken quite a fancy to you in that mask. Mysterious, scary and a little forbidden. I hope you have it with you for one final performance?'

He reached into his pocket and produced the dark blue hood. We both grinned as the door closed with a click and a promise . . .

16

Spring 1878

'Good morning, Grace. Not long to go for the blessed event, now?'

'Two months or thereabouts. Long enough,' I smiled. It was to be a happy time for me, the birth of my first child. I prayed that Seb would be around and not gallivanting over his division.

It had been a compromise, him leaving the newly formed Criminal Investigation Bureau in Sydney as a Senior Detective to return to uniform. True, he was now the Divisional Commander for all the troopers from Wagga Wagga to Broken Hill but with the new railways as well as Cobb and Co, he was not away that much.

It was his insistence to be based here and, having smashed the New Eden conspiracy, his outrageous request was granted.

There had never been much publicity

concerning the arrests and incarceration of the twenty or so ring-leaders. Top-secret. Not even trial by jury. Treason had its special rules.

Perhaps in the not too distant future, my husband and I would return to Sydney for him to head up the fledgling elite police force there. For now, however, Jerilderie was our home.

Without the toxic atmosphere of Grenville Younger, the town has flourished, both Elmer and Herman Younger showing themselves to be dedicated and capable officers in the New South Wales police. They were soon to be promoted and move to Hay and Narrandera respectively.

★ ★ ★

'Might I enquire as to where Divisional Superintendent Longstreet is at the moment, Grace?' Ma Huxley asked.

I mopped my brow with a cotton handkerchief. It was uncomfortably warm this time of the year and my confinement did not help.

'Wagga Wagga. There are problems with a gang led by Ned Kelly crossing from Victoria to our colony.'

'Kelly? Wasn't he the gentleman who visited Mr Younger that first week you taught? The one fascinated with the knights of old and their armour?'

I laughed. 'Yes. You have a fine memory Ma. A strange fascination by a strange man, although he was pleasant enough to me.'

The school was going well though I would soon have to step aside for my pupil-teacher who would continue under my tutelage. A teenage boy was starting on Monday, a bit of a larrikin by all accounts.

I was keen to meet him and to show him that I was not some weak woman to boss around — although boxing was presently out of the question.

'Tell me, Ma Huxley. What of you and Mr Applegate?' I asked, teasingly. 'Are all your wedding preparations progressing well?'

'Exceedingly so, Grace — Oh! The time. I must take my leave. Take care of yourself — and the baby. From what I hear, there are changes afoot for our fine country and its future and I hope to witness them.'

'What changes?'

'We have six colonies in our continent and my Mr Applegate has been talking with a very learned gentleman regarding a confederation of those colonies to form a brand new country!

'Of course, it might take years to get the governments to agree but would it not be a wonderful thing, Grace?'

'It would, indeed.'

A new country? There would be one name for it above all others. Our continent of Terra Australis would be Australia.

What a wonderful event to look forward to.

We do hope that you have enjoyed reading this large print book.

Did you know that all of our titles are available for purchase?

We publish a wide range of high quality large print books including:
Romances, Mysteries, Classics
General Fiction
Non Fiction and Westerns

Special interest titles available in large print are:
The Little Oxford Dictionary
Music Book, Song Book
Hymn Book, Service Book

Also available from us courtesy of Oxford University Press:
Young Readers' Dictionary
(large print edition)
Young Readers' Thesaurus
(large print edition)

For further information or a free brochure, please contact us at:
Ulverscroft Large Print Books Ltd.,
The Green, Bradgate Road, Anstey,
Leicester, LE7 7FU, England.
Tel: (00 44) 0116 236 4325
Fax: (00 44) 0116 234 0205

Other titles in the
Linford Romance Library:

HER HEART TO WIN

Jasmina Svenne

When the rakishly handsome Jem Hale impudently accosts the demure schoolteacher Marianne in the street, little do either of them know what dramatic repercussions their meeting — and a drunken bet among Jem and his acquaintances — will have on their lives. Not to mention the effects upon those in their wider social circle too . . .